Dear Reader,

We're thrilled that some of Harlequin's most famous families are making an encore appearance! With this special Famous Families fifty-book collection, we are proud to offer you the chance to relive the drama, the glamour, the suspense and the romance of four of Harlequin's most beloved families— the Fortunes, the Bravos, the McCabes and the Cavanaughs.

You'll begin your journey at the Double Crown ranch in Red Rock, Texas, home of the legendary Fortunes and the setting of the twelve-book miniseries Fortunes of Texas: Reunion. Members of the family are preparing to honor their patriarch, Ryan Fortune, but a bloodred moon offers a portent of trouble ahead. As the clan deals with a mysterious body, an abduction, a health crisis and numerous family secrets, each member also manages to find love and a happily-ever-after you'll want to share.

We hope you enjoy your time in Red Rock. Be prepared for our next stop, the Rising Sun Ranch in Medicine Creek, Wyoming, where *USA TODAY* bestselling author Christine Rimmer kicks off the story of the Bravo family. Watch for *The Nine-Month Marriage,* the first of the Bravo series, beginning in March!

Happy reading,

The Editors

CHRISTIE RIDGWAY

Native Californian Christie Ridgway started reading and writing romances in middle school. It wasn't until she was the wife of her college sweetheart and the mother of two small sons that she submitted her work for publication. Many contemporary romances later, she is the happiest when telling her stories despite the splash of kids in the pool, the mass of cups and plates in the kitchen and the many commitments she makes in the world beyond her desk.

Besides loving the men in her life and her dream-come-true job, she continues her longtime love affair with reading and is never without a stack of books.

You can find out more about Christie at her website, www.christieridgway.com.

FAMOUS FAMILIES

the FORTUNES

USA TODAY bestselling author

CHRISTIE RIDGWAY

The Reckoning

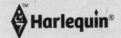

Harlequin®

TORONTO NEW YORK LONDON
AMSTERDAM PARIS SYDNEY HAMBURG
STOCKHOLM ATHENS TOKYO MILAN MADRID
PRAGUE WARSAW BUDAPEST AUCKLAND

Special thanks and acknowledgment are given to Christie Ridgway for her contribution to the Fortunes of Texas: Reunion series.

To the other authors on the Fortunes of Texas: Reunion loop who have made this project such fun.

Recycling programs
for this product may
not exist in your area.

ISBN-13: 978-0-373-36491-6

THE RECKONING

FAMOUS FAMILIES

The Fortunes

The Bravos by Christine Rimmer

Chapter 1

Inside the rambling Texas ranch house were a profusion of flowers, tables groaning with food and two bars stocked with plenty of liquor. All the makings of one hell of a great party, Emmett Jamison thought from the shadowed corner where he stood. That is, if the guest of honor hadn't been dead.

"I can't believe he's gone," he overheard a tiny, gray-haired lady by a punch bowl say to her companion. "I just can't believe that Ryan Fortune is gone."

Emmett's eyes closed. He wished he couldn't believe it. But the older man had been diagnosed with a brain tumor several months before and despite his big, vital personality and all the family and friends who cared about him, just that morning Ryan Fortune's ashes had been spread across the lands of his beloved Double Crown Ranch.

The tragedy of it didn't surprise Emmett. All hope

and optimism had been swept out of him months ago. He expected no happy endings. He was becoming accustomed to funerals.

"Trying out for the undertaker's job?" a new voice murmured in his ear. "You've got the morose expression for it."

"I don't take offense at your ugly mug," he answered automatically, "so you shouldn't take offense at my unsmiling one."

The "ugly" insult didn't have much meat to it, though, not when the man who had come up beside him was his cousin, Collin Jamison, and not when all agreed that Collin was a slightly older version of Emmett himself. They were both six feet tall and had the solid build of men whose fitness and training kept them employed—and alive. They wore their dark hair in no-nonsense military cuts, and Collin's hazel eyes were only a touch lighter than Emmett's green ones.

"You're not offending me," Collin replied. "You're worrying me. You've got that let-me-escape-to-the-mountains look about you."

Emmett shoved his hands into the pockets of his dark trousers. He'd holed himself up in the Sandia Mountains of New Mexico following his brother Christopher's funeral last September and the tragic ending to one of his FBI cases. There, he'd tried deadening himself to that pain and all that had come before with cheap tequila and stubborn solitude. Neither had lasted long enough. When his father had brought the news that his other brother, Jason, who had been implicated in Chris's murder, had escaped from jail, Emmett had sobered up and returned to Texas. "When Dad found me in New Mexico, he confiscated the keys to the cabin and threatened to burn the place down." Though lack of keys wouldn't stop anyone from getting into that shack. "I won't be going back there."

"Good," Collin said, then surveyed the crowded room. "I haven't seen Uncle Blake and Aunt Darcy, but it's wall-to-wall people. Are they here?"

Emmett shook his head. "I'm the sole representative of our branch of the Jamisons. Mom and Dad didn't feel comfortable attending, considering their son was the one who kidnapped Ryan's widow just a couple of months back." Jason's kidnapping of Lily Fortune was what had brought his cousin Collin to Red Rock, Texas. Emmett had called him after the older woman's recovery and his brother's escape. Emmett had wanted Collin's help in stopping Jason. That job wasn't done.

Collin seemed to read his mind. "We're going to get him, Emmett."

"*I'm* going to get him," Emmett corrected, though he and the authorities on the case were fresh out of leads and they all knew it. Though Lily had been recovered, Jason had taken off with the ransom money, killing an FBI agent in the process. There hadn't been a sign of him since.

"You have Lucy to focus on now, Collin. But come hell or high water, I'm not going to let my brother make a victim of anyone else." Jason's ugly criminal tally also included the death of his own girlfriend, Melissa, and that of a prison transport guard. Though a prison guard in on Jason's plan—McGruder—had been arrested and would stand trial for his part in the escape, it wasn't nearly enough justice. Emmett's voice lowered. "If it's the last thing I do, I'm going to make Jason pay for all the pain he's caused."

"You're going grim on me again, buddy," Collin

warned softly. "By all means, let's get Jason safely behind bars, but not at the cost of your heart."

Emmett had to shake his head at that. Falling in love with Lucy had done a number on his tough-natured cousin. "Romance has made you soft. You know I don't have a heart."

And Emmett didn't feel like talking about it anymore, either. Without bothering to make an excuse, he wandered away from his cousin, avoiding the eyes of those around him. Turning a corner, he almost knocked over an easel that held a poster-size photo. He reached out a hand to steady the smiling image of Ryan Fortune. "Husband, Father, Friend" was printed on the cardboard beneath it. "Loved By All."

Emmett's fingers lingered on the edge of the poster. Ryan's eyes seemed to glitter as they had in life, and then Emmett felt a warm weight on his shoulder, as if the man were holding him there with a ghostly hand. To tell him something? To remind him of something?

Struck by a new, vague disquiet, Emmett hurried off, heading for the ranch house's foyer. He pushed open the heavy front door, undeterred by a blast of chilly April wind. The sky was as dark as his mood and it smelled like rain, but he needed fresh air. More, he needed to be alone. He didn't need a reminder of what he owed Ryan.

Loved By All. That phrase flitted into Emmett's mind as he stepped outside. His brother Chris's headstone read Beloved. Jessica Chandler's family had carved In Loving Memory onto hers.

The past few years had taught that those stock phrases didn't solve one damn thing, though. They didn't make it any easier for the living to carry on.

Love didn't make it any easier for the living to carry on. And love certainly didn't wake the dead.

Oblivious to the cool temperature, he leaned against one wall of the covered entryway, staring at the terracotta pots filled with flowers that lined the stone walkway in front of him. A few brave blooms were already showing their faces, but in May the April showers would really pay off. Emmett wondered if he'd still be in Red Rock to see it—and then admitted to himself he more than likely wouldn't notice if he were. It had been winter inside him for what seemed like aeons now.

From around the corner of the entryway, a soft, rhythmic *thup thup thup* caught his attention. Curious, he shoved his hands deeper in his pockets and drifted down the steps to take a look at what was making the noise.

It was a kid, medium-size, in an expensive navy blazer and a pair of khakis with a streak of mud on one knee. Between his shiny loafers was a fist-size, black-and-white ball that the boy tossed upward with one foot three times, *thup thup thup,* before it fell to the stone pathway and he had to start all over again, lifting it with his toe, juggling it for a few moments then losing it again.

Emmett's mind flashed back three months, maybe four. Then, he'd seen that same child, in a diner in Red Rock, sitting with an older couple and across from a blonde woman. Emmett had only seen the blonde's back but he'd seen the tension on the boy's face.

A gust of wind tossed the kid's blond bangs around his forehead and shook a few raindrops out of the low clouds above. The kid looked up, shivered, but went back to his game. The next blast of cold wind started the rain in earnest. Emmett stepped back toward the front door, almost calling to the boy to come inside, but then he shrugged. Hell, the kid wasn't his concern.

He had other priorities.

Behind him, he heard the door open. "Richard?" a female voice called. "Richard, are you out there?"

The kid ducked his head and kept juggling the ball, despite the rain and despite the person obviously seeking him out. Shrugging again, Emmett turned toward the entryway. He'd wanted fresh air, not a fresh soaking. It was time to go back inside, find Lily and mumble some more condolences, then leave.

"Richard?" The voice floated closer.

And then, from around the corner of the house, a woman came into view.

And brought out the sun.

It was just the capricious spring weather, Emmett knew that, but it halted him midstride anyway as a warm beam of light broke through the clouds to spotlight the woman's long blond hair, her soft white dress, her slender, delicate body.

He blinked. She was an angel, a candle, a…

A sign that he needed to get more than three hours of sleep a night, he thought, disgusted. Her gaze bounced off Emmett and then zeroed in on the boy.

"Richard—"

"Ricky, I keep telling you," the kid muttered. "Ricky, Ricky, Ricky."

The woman's forehead wrinkled and Emmett wondered if she might actually cry. He took a step toward her, driven by the sudden thought that he should comfort her, care for her, something, but then she squared her shoulders and her mouth turned up in a little half smile.

"Well, Ricky-Ricky-Ricky, you shouldn't be outside in the rain."

"It's not raining anymore."

Emmett said that. He couldn't believe he'd insinuated himself into the strangers' conversation. But then again, he couldn't believe that odd compulsion he'd had to take the woman into his arms, either. More sleep was definitely a necessity.

The woman shot him a puzzled glance, then tipped her face to the sky, like one of those flowers he'd been looking at before. Light bathed her features, illuminating her clear pale skin, her small nose and her pretty mouth.

He thought of springtime again, actually *remembered* springtime, with its warmth and sweet scents and green newness. His feet took another step closer to her before he stopped them.

"I guess you're right. It isn't raining anymore," she said, closing her eyes. She swayed a bit, as if slightly unbalanced. "Doesn't the sunshine feel good?"

Emmett refused to answer the question; instead, he asked, "Who are you?" Immediately, he was aware he sounded abrupt and hostile—quite a feat for someone as naturally abrupt and hostile as himself. But the woman unsettled him, ruffled him somehow, and he wanted to figure out what it was, exactly, she did to him. And why.

To his surprise, it was the truculent kid who answered. While he had seemed peeved at the woman himself, now he moved to stand between her and Emmett, a purely protective stance. "She's Linda Faraday," the boy said. "I'm Ricky. Who are *you?*"

Linda Faraday. Her son, Ricky. Emmett's gut tightened. He'd forgotten about them in the days since

Ryan's death. Perhaps it explained the disquiet he'd felt when looking at the older man's photo. And perhaps it was why he'd reacted so strongly to the woman a few minutes before—his subconscious had recognized her and remembered his promise. Not the one he'd made *for* Ryan, about capturing Jason, but that promise he'd made *to* Ryan.

"Well?" the kid said. "Who are you?"

Emmett took in a long breath, then gazed into Linda Faraday's wide blue eyes. *Springtime.* He had to shove the thought away before it derailed him. "I'm the man who's going to be looking after you," he told her.

Back inside the house, Emmett didn't waste any time. Rather than wandering about, Emmett asked the first person he knew if he'd seen Dr. Violet Fortune. That person had, and Emmett strode through the somber crowds to find Dr. Fortune in the dining room, putting fruit salad on a small plate.

"I need some of your time, Violet," he told her.

She set down the silver serving spoon, then turned and studied his face. "What you need is more rest, less guilt and a good meal or two. That'll be two hundred dollars. You can mail a check to my home office."

"Ha-ha." He didn't crack a smile. "I want to talk to you about Linda Faraday."

"Oh, well, I'm not her doctor, and even if I were, I couldn't—"

"Ryan spoke to you about her, didn't he?" Linda Faraday and her son, Ricky, had been Ryan's source of guilt for over a decade, thanks to the car accident caused by his brother, Cameron, who had been driving drunk. Cameron had died in that accident, and Linda, his passenger, had been terribly hurt. Ryan had kept that secret from the public and from his family, except for Lily and Violet. Linda had been pregnant with Cameron's child. That boy was Ricky.

Violet gave a little nod. "Ryan talked about her situation more than a time or two, but it was with the understanding that the situation was confidential. I wouldn't feel right discussing—"

"Discuss traumatic brain injury with me, then." Because that was what Linda Faraday had suffered ten years before. "And discuss comas and recovery and rehabilitation and—"

"Okay, okay." Violet put a cool hand on his arm. "Am I to assume you mean you want to discuss these things now?"

Maybe he should have felt guilty for insisting, but he didn't. He'd felt helpless in the face of Ryan's death and stymied in discovering Jason's whereabouts, but here was something, finally, he could take action on. "Yes, now. Please," he added as an afterthought.

Half smiling and shaking her head, Violet patted his arm. "How about we meet in the study after I give Peter a heads-up? Celeste is at home, so we didn't plan on staying long."

Emmett grimaced. Celeste was the little girl that Peter and Violet were adopting, and she'd recently gone through serious back surgery and rehabilitation of her own. "Tell your husband I'll make it as brief as I can."

Violet gave another shake of her head and another half smile. "You're not long-winded, I can say that for you, Emmett."

Which meant he was brusque to a fault. But he could live with that, especially when Violet got back to him so quickly. Emmett had secured a private place for their chat on a short leather sofa in a far corner of the study.

When she settled beside him, he took his eyes off the massive burl wood desk at one end of the room. "The last time I was in here, Ryan seemed to take up more space than that desk of his," he murmured.

Violet handed him one of two cups of coffee she held. "We're all trying to grasp the fact that Ryan's gone."

But Emmett, on the other hand, was going to do something about it. He couldn't bring the man back, of course, but he could follow through with the pledge he'd made to him. "Traumatic brain injury," he prompted without more ado.

"I just love these little social niceties of yours, Emmett," Violet said, grimacing. Then she seemed to take pity on him. "All right. I'll stop wasting your time. Traumatic brain injury."

She sipped from her cup, then began. "Otherwise known as TBI, or head injury, it's simply damage to the brain caused by an external force. It's common in vehicle accidents, when impact can cause the brain to bounce back and forth against the skull. That causes bruising to the brain and, later, swelling. Head injuries are the number-one killer of Americans under the age of forty-four. They kill more under the age of thirty-four than all diseases combined."

Emmett absorbed the numbers, but at the moment only one person with a head injury mattered to him. "Do all people with a TBI go into a coma?"

"Serious injury can occur without a loss of consciousness, but in a TBI, usually the brain stem is injured and that produces a period of coma that may last for some time."

"But in a coma for *years?* Is that usual, Violet?"

The good doctor hesitated, because, Emmett knew,

they were getting into Linda Faraday–specific territory. She'd gone into a coma following the car accident. Then the doctors had discovered she was a couple of months pregnant. She'd given birth in that state and stayed in that state until a little over a year ago.

"What's more unusual, Emmett," Violet finally said, "is for a patient to recover enough to make an independent life for herself after so long."

"It's not like the movies, huh? Snoozing away until one day the patient awakes, refreshed and alert?"

Violet shook her head. "Maybe for Sleeping Beauty, but in the real world that doesn't happen. In the case of Linda—" She stopped herself. "Emmett, I don't feel right about this."

He didn't waste his breath arguing with her. "Let's talk hypotheticals, then. If a hypothetical patient were in a coma…"

Violet was shaking her head again.

"She wasn't in a coma?"

"The technical definition of a coma is an altered state of consciousness in which the patient's eyes don't open and the patient doesn't react to pain or commands, or doesn't speak in recognizable words. So while the hypothetical patient might start out that way, once she can react, respond or speak, then she's no longer in a coma, though she may not yet be returned to full consciousness. In that semiconscious state, patients can be fed, or feed themselves, and get some kinds of physical therapy to keep their muscles from atrophying. There are people who remain in that twilight state for the rest of their lives."

"So what brought Linda out of—excuse me—what might bring a hypothetical patient out of that twilight and into full consciousness?"

Violet shrugged. "No one knows. After so many years, I suppose the best explanation is...a miracle."

He frowned at that, *miracle* not being in the vocabulary of a been-there, seen-every-horror FBI agent. "Ryan seemed to think that Linda still needs some kind of help. I promised to provide that."

Violet opened her mouth, closed it, then sighed. "All right. Linda. Let's talk about Linda. Ryan was right that she'll need help. Ten years have passed. The world isn't the same as Linda remembers. *She's* not the same as she remembers. She's been in a rehab facility for the past year, relearning old skills and acquiring new skills to cope with those ways in which she's changed, but it can't be easy."

"Ryan said she was being released from rehab soon. He wanted me to...protect her."

"That sounds like Ryan. But you'll have to find out from Linda if protection is what she wants—or will accept. From what I understand, she'll be going to the home of Nancy and Dean Armstrong, the couple who have taken care of Ricky since infancy."

Emmett thought of the truculent Ricky and the ethereal Linda. "It doesn't matter what she wants. I promised Ryan. It's the least I can do for him."

"There's that guilt again," Violet said. "Any woman, even one who has been in Linda's shoes, won't appreciate being an obligation to you."

"She's not an obligation. She's a..." Compulsion. The light. Springtime. In his mind's eye, he saw her face turned up to the sunshine and again he felt that warm weight of Ryan's hand on his shoulder. She needed him, and he was being directed to take care of her. God, how could he explain it to Violet without her calling for the men in white coats with straitjackets? "She's just something I know I'm supposed to do right now."

Violet toasted him with a little dip of her coffee cup. "Then good luck convincing her of that."

Linda consulted the notebook on her bedside table the moment she woke up. It was chubby, with a no-nonsense blue tagboard cover. Today's place was marked with a simple paper clip. She read the words she'd penciled in the evening before to aid her in those first, often confusing moments of awakening.

Today is Tuesday, May 2.
YOUR ROOM HAS MOVED.
You live in the south wing now. Bathroom is on the right.
If it's morning, get up, shower, dress. Go to breakfast.
Turn left for the dining hall.

Tuesday, May 2. The date hadn't been a revelation, though the year might take her an instant or two to conjure up. She was even already aware that her room had moved. But she still kept up the habits that had gotten her through the first months at the rehabilitation facility, when blinking could cause her to lose her train of thought—or worse, a day or two of short-term memories.

She stretched, then climbed out of bed and took in the outfit she'd laid out for herself the night before. Yoga pants, T-shirt, running shoes. She had physical therapy scheduled for the late morning, which meant time on the elliptical machine and stretching on the mats. A year ago, she'd been learning to walk again; these days, she was itching to take a run on the sidewalk.

In a few days, she might do just that.

At the thought, anxiety tripped up her heart. She ignored the feeling, though, and continued into the bathroom. The rehab facility was a comfortable, comforting place, but her counselors assured her she was ready to move out into the big, bad world.

She wished they wouldn't refer to it like that. They meant it as a joke, of course, but she didn't find it all that funny.

In the big, bad world, she had to create a new life for herself. An independent life…well, as independent as a life could be that also contained the ten-year-old who was her son, Richard. Ricky.

She thought of him and the corners of her lips tipped up as she stepped under the shower spray. He might scare her to death—he *did* scare her to death—but he could still make her smile. Her fingers closed around the bar of oatmeal soap, and she brought it against her body.

And froze.

"Damn, damn, damn," she muttered, slamming the bar back into place. Then she reached toward her knees and grasped the wet hem of her sopping nightshirt to pull it over her head. It landed in the bottom of the shower stall with a *splat.*

The small mistake put her in lousy mood that the bright dining hall and the excellent breakfast menu couldn't dissipate. One of the rehab counselors noted it, apparently, because she came to sit beside Linda during her second cup of coffee.

"Bad dreams? Headache?" she asked.

Those were a couple of lingering ailments, but not

today's problem. Linda felt heat warm her cheeks. "Showered in my nightgown."

The counselor smiled. "Is that all?"

"Isn't that enough? What kind of grown woman steps under the spray of the shower wearing her clothes? It's bad enough that I have to have routines to remind myself to wash and rinse my hair. Now I'm forgetting to get naked first."

The woman leaned closer. "Don't tell anyone, but once I came to work in my pink fuzzy slippers. When we have a lot on our minds, sometimes we let the simple things slip by."

But how was she supposed to be independent, let alone a mother, if she couldn't remember the simple things?

The other woman must have read the question on her face. "You handled the situation, didn't you, Linda? You recognized the error, coped with it. That's all any of us can ask of ourselves."

Linda had never been a whiner, but still… "It was a *shower*," she muttered. "You'd think I could get that right."

"Is there something else bothering you, Linda? Some worry? You know that can put you off your game."

Linda drummed her fingertips against the tabletop. A few months back, she hadn't had the dexterity to do such a thing. The hours of drilling with computer games had paid off. "It's…it's a man," she admitted.

"Ryan Fortune?" The counselor rubbed Linda's shoulder. "Grief is perfectly normal, too."

Linda gave a vague nod. She *did* grieve for Ryan. He'd been a gentle friend to her, like a kindly uncle, and he'd given her a much-needed anchor in those first months after she came fully, miraculously conscious. It had been Ryan who had found this wonderful facility, and had paid for it. It had been Ryan who, she learned a few days after his death, had set up trusts for both herself and her son that gave them financial security for the rest of their lives.

"But it's a different man I'm thinking of," she told the counselor. Her hand automatically reached for her notebook and flipped it open to the most recent page. It was what she'd written after the breakfast reminder.

9:00 a.m., you have a meeting with the Armstrongs…

The Armstrongs were another miracle in her life. After Ricky's birth, Ryan had met the couple through the Mothers Against Drunk Driving organization. They'd lost their daughter, son-in-law and granddaughter to a drunk driver. Learning of what had befallen Linda, they'd opened their home to Ricky and their hearts to his mother, as well, even though for long years she hadn't been aware of their weekly visits or their prayers and hopes for her recovery. They were going to bring her to their house when she was released from rehab and assured her that she and Ricky had a place with them for as long as she liked. She knew they regarded her as a daughter and Ricky as their treasured grandson.

The Armstrongs didn't worry her.

9:00 a.m., you have a meeting with the Armstrongs and Emmett Jamison.

Emmett Jamison. Now *he* worried her. Her finger nervously tapped the page beneath his name.

"Who's Emmett Jamison?" the counselor asked.

"*What* is more like it," Linda said under her breath. FBI agent. Tough guy. So take-charge he had made her feel flustered, hot and confused with just one level look from those searing green eyes of his. A woman who'd been half-asleep for so many years didn't have one technique on hand to cope with *him*.

The day they'd met, he'd been adamant about who he was. "I'm the man who's going to be looking after you," he'd said, then stalked off, leaving her staring. She would have dismissed him as a loony or some figment of her misfiring memory if Ricky hadn't discovered the intriguing FBI agent, tough-guy tidbits from some others attending Ryan's memorial. And then yesterday, Emmett had phoned to tell her he'd arranged to speak with her and the Armstrongs. She had no idea why. She was afraid to guess.

"Linda, who is this man?" the counselor prodded.

"Emmett Jamison is…" Her hand lifted. "Emmett Jamison is…"

"Early," filled in a deep voice from the doorway of the dining room.

Linda shivered, because there he was, staring at her with those intense green eyes of his and looking dark and determined. A big, bad wolf from the big, bad world.

Chapter 2

Linda discovered that the hallways of the rehab facility weren't wide enough when Emmett Jamison was walking by her side. He seemed so big, so male, in his casual slacks and open-throated dress shirt. It wasn't as if he tried to crowd her, but he just seemed to be so close, so *there,* as she led the way toward her room.

He was loud, too. Not in the usual sense—as a matter of fact, he didn't even make an attempt at small talk—but the quiet way he moved, the confident aura attached to him, made his very presence noisy. There was no way to ignore someone like that.

She couldn't wait to get rid of him.

"You didn't say why you wanted to meet with me," she ventured. If she hadn't been so surprised and confused when he'd called the day before, she would have insisted on finding out the reason then.

"I didn't?" His expression remained unreadable as

he glanced into one of the rehab classrooms. Three of the center's clients sat at different tables, one working on a computer game, another inserting pegs in a Peg-Board, another putting together a simple puzzle. "Is that the kind of thing you've been doing the past year?" he asked.

"Yes," Linda answered. There was no point in pretending otherwise. "Computer games and puzzles to improve dexterity and memory and focus. And then there have been sessions of physical therapy, speech therapy and occupational therapy. In many respects— most, maybe—I was like a child when I came here. There was a lot I had to relearn."

"But now you're... What would you call it? Up to speed? Cured?"

Anxiety washed over Linda again like a cold sweat. "I'll never be cured," she admitted. It was the hard truth that the rehab center tried to make the head-injured understand. "I'm a different person now than I was before the car accident."

But exactly who was that new person? The question was only exacerbated by the decade that she'd lost. With her past nearly as hazy as her future, she continued to struggle with developing her identity—even believing that she could. Leaving the rehab center, she worried, would only make that problem more overwhelming.

More frightening.

Finding Nancy and Dean Armstrong already waiting in the small sitting area of her room didn't ease the feeling. They were wonderful, generous people who had always cared for Ricky and her, including visiting her regularly during her rehab and taking her out on day trips around the area and to their San Antonio home. But seeing them today only served to remind her that soon, so soon, she would be moving into their household and she would be expected to not only begin making a life for herself, but begin making herself into a mother for her son.

"Nancy, Dean. It's good to see you." Linda exchanged brief hugs with them.

"I brought more pictures." Nancy pressed a packet of snapshots into her hand. "Soccer photos and some from the field trip I chaperoned last week."

Linda's fingers tightened on the pictures. The Armstrongs were so conscientious about integrating her into Ricky's life. They shared photos and stories and the boy's company at every opportunity. It wasn't their fault she had trouble accepting herself as a mother.

Ducking the thought, she gestured toward her companion. "And do you two know Emmett Jamison?"

They apparently did, which puzzled Linda even more. So with everyone seated, she decided to get the situation straightened out. "Mr. Jamison—"

"Emmett," he corrected.

"Emmett, then. What can I—" she looked at the older couple "—what can *we* do for you?"

On the love seat across from the straight chairs that she and Emmett were seated upon, Nancy and Dean exchanged glances. The big, bad wolf kept his gaze trained on her. "It's what I can do for you."

She did *not* like the way he said the words. She did not. "But I don't need anything."

Emmett's gaze flicked toward Nancy and Dean. "You'll be leaving the rehab facility shortly. I want to be a help to you."

Was he offering his services as a mover? That was the only thing that made any sense. "I'm going to be living at the Armstrongs' house, and I have very little to bring with me there from here. Some clothes, a few books, that's all."

He didn't answer right away, leaving a silence to well in the room. Her stomach gave a nervous jump, and she withdrew the photos from their envelope to give her fingers something to do. The glossy images fanned across her lap.

"I promised Ryan," the man said.

She frowned. "Promised him what?"

"That I'd look after you. That I'd do what I could to make things easier for you." He finally looked away from her face. "I've made a couple of promises, and I intend to keep them."

Oh-kay. "That was very…nice of Ryan, and typical of him to be worried about me, but I don't need to be looked after. I don't need anyone to make things easier." Well, of course she did, but she doubted there was a person in the universe who could make her feel like a real mother and a complete woman instead of the jumble of unconnected puzzle pieces she regarded as herself.

"More convenient, then," he put in. "I could make things more convenient for you."

Uncertain how to reject his offer, she looked over at the Armstrongs in mute appeal. It was then she read the worried expression on Nancy's face. "What is it?" she asked. "What aren't you telling me?"

The older woman sighed. "I think we're all confusing you, Linda, and we certainly don't mean to do that. It's just that we came up with a new plan that we thought might work out better for you."

"A new plan? A new plan that involves *him?*" She pointed at Emmett. "Now I really am confused."

Dean cleared his throat. "When Emmett contacted us about his promise to Ryan, we thought his offer was a timely one. It presents an opportunity for you to gain a greater degree of independence than you could find if you simply moved into our home. You know your counselors weren't sure that was such a good idea."

Linda swallowed. She knew full well that the counselors at the rehab facility weren't one hundred percent behind her move to the Armstrongs'. The couple had household help—a housekeeper, a cook. With all that available assistance, there was a worry that Linda might not get enough practice at the life skills she'd been working so hard on during the past year.

"You think I shouldn't move in with you?" Her voice came out almost a whisper. If the Armstrongs cut her loose, could she put the pieces of herself together? Could she take care of Ricky *and* forge together a Linda Faraday?

"No, no, Linda. We want you with us," Nancy hastened to say. "What we're proposing is that you move into the guest house beyond the pool. It has three bedrooms, a bath-and-a-half, a full kitchen. There, you'd have the chance to take care of yourself, from grocery shopping to cooking. Emmett could stay in one of the other bedrooms, as a…a backup, say, for the first few weeks."

Linda rubbed her forehead and the throbbing beginning to grow there. Changes—of plans, of routines, even of the faces that surrounded her—could throw her off. Adapting to new ideas and situations was one of those life skills that she was supposed to work on as she moved into her new life.

She looked down, her gaze landing on the photos in her lap. A dozen or so pictures of kids, one in particular. She was so disconcerted, it took her a moment to realize what she was seeing. Whom.

Ricky. Of course, Ricky. Moving down the soccer field. With his arm around two other boys. Pointing at some out-of-focus exhibit in a museum. Not just some anonymous little boy, but Ricky. Ricky, her son.

Dean must have noticed the direction of her gaze. "While you're getting your bearings in the guest house, he would remain in his own room in our home, Linda, but visit with you as often as he likes, of course. It could be the best of both worlds."

The best of both worlds. The phrase stuck in her head. The best of both worlds. The best.

The best part of the whole idea of moving into the guest house, the most *tempting* part, was that it would allow her more distance and more time. More distance from her scariest fear. More time, she thought, shame and relief intertwining, to not be Ricky's mother.

Her mind made up, she didn't bother glancing over at Emmett again. It wasn't noble, it wasn't brave, but it was the truth. She would even put up with the big, bad wolf if he'd get between her and the big, bad world of being a mother to her child.

Today is Friday, May 8.
YOU HAVE MOVED.
You live in the Armstrongs' guest house now.
Bathroom is across the hall.
If it's morning, get up, shower, dress.

The few lines in her notebook cut through the anxiety of awakening in an unfamiliar bed in an unfamiliar room. Her mind easy again, she watched the play of sunlight over the yellow-and-violet wallpapered walls. She'd moved her belongings into the pretty little room the afternoon before, and then, worn out by the excitement and the change of scenery, had put on her nightwear, stretched out on the bed and promptly fallen asleep. Luckily, she'd remembered to pencil in the next day's pertinent info before heading for dreamland at the early hour of 6:00 p.m.

Her stomach growled, a reminder that she hadn't eaten since yesterday's lunch. Food would wait, though.

If it's morning, get up, shower, dress.

She found it simpler to follow the instructions in her notebook. Improvisation could lead to disaster, like the time she'd ignored the direction to dress before her morning appointment. She'd showed up for a meeting with one of Ryan Fortune's attorneys in baby-doll pajamas. Lucky for her, it had been in a conference room at the rehab center, rather than a downtown San Antonio law office.

Climbing out of bed, she noted she was wearing those very same baby dolls. Nancy had picked them out, as she'd picked out most of Linda's limited wardrobe. These were a pale peach, thin cotton. Little shorts barely covered her rear, while the top was sleeveless, with tiny pintucks on the bodice. She made a face at her reflected image in the mirror over the dresser on the other side of the room. Her body was still too thin, and the childish pajamas made her look twelve instead of thirty-three.

In addition to having the figure of a preteen, the years she'd been semiconscious didn't show on her skin. She had the complexion of a twentysomething, and she supposed she should be grateful for that.

Her stomach growled again.

Shower, dress, she reminded herself again. *Bathroom is across the hall.*

As she pushed open the bedroom door, the door across the hall—the bathroom door—opened.

A man stood before her.

Her mouth dropped, but no sound came out. He was big. Big and naked, except for a pale green towel wrapped low on his hips. Damp, curling hair was scattered across his wide chest and more of the stuff created a thin line between rippling abdominal muscles. As she stared, steam curled out from behind him. He looked like an erotic genie emerging from a bathroom-size bottle.

Too late, she crossed her arms over the thin cotton that covered her breasts.

Not that he was looking at them. Instead, he was studying her face, his body perfectly still, as if she were a wild animal he was trying not to startle.

"Good morning," he said softly. "I thought you were still asleep."

She took a step back.

He went even stiller, if that was possible. "I'm Emmett, do you remember?"

"Of course I remember," she scoffed, taking another step back into the bedroom. Then she slammed the door shut between them.

She *did* remember who he was. But in the confusion of the move, she'd forgotten something else. She reached for her pencil and her notebook and sat down on the edge of the mattress. There, she scratched out some lines she'd written and wrote some new ones.

YOU HAVE MOVED.
You live in the Armstrongs' guest house now

WITH EMMETT JAMISON. Bathroom is across
the hall AND REALIZE THAT HE MIGHT BE
IN THERE AHEAD OF YOU.
If it's morning, get up, shower, dress.
DON'T FORGET TO WEAR A ROBE.

Her turn in the shower gave her time to reabsorb the
fact that she had a housemate. The small tiled enclosure
retained a masculine scent that she found not unpleas-
ant, and she was happy to see that he hadn't rearranged
the various bottles that she'd set upon the high window
ledge.

After adjusting the spray and getting inside—
making sure she was properly naked—she removed
the red cap of the shampoo, the blue cap of the condi-
tioner and the yellow cap of the finishing rinse. As she
completed using each one, she'd replace the cap. That
way, by the shower's end, she'd be certain she'd completed her hair routine and not emerge with a head of
soapsuds as she'd done a time or two before.

The little ritual freed her concentration to focus on
Emmett again. He was going to act as her net for her
first four weeks of living in the Armstrongs' guest
house. If she "fell" in any way, he was supposed to be
there to catch her. To that end, she'd given him permission to talk to her rehab counselors about what to
expect during this transition period. It was embarrass-
ing, but she'd had plenty of practice dealing with embarrassment in the past months.

It wasn't as if he was really a man. Not to her,
anyway. To her he was a tool, that was all. While
they lived together, she'd consider him like…another
appliance. Blow-dryer, toaster, Emmett Jamison. An

appliance that appeared incredibly sexy when he was half-naked, sure, but an appliance all the same.

It wasn't as if he appeared impressed with, or even aware of, her femaleness, which only made it simpler to overlook the fact that he was a living, breathing, very attractive male specimen. It made it easier to face him, too, when she found him in the kitchen after she'd finished her shower and changed into a pair of jeans, T-shirt and running shoes.

"Coffee?" he offered, standing beside the counter-top, a glass carafe in his hand.

Appliance, all right, she thought, suppressing a smile. She took the mug he held out to her with a murmured thanks. Then they both sat down at the small kitchen table. He pulled a section of the newspaper toward him at the same time that he pushed a heaping basket of fruit toward her.

She took a banana as he proceeded to read. Yes, her very own vending machine, one that dispensed coffee and fruit at convenient intervals. She could get used to this.

Then she thought with an interior grimace, she *was* used to this. One of the reasons she was supposed to live independently was to learn to do for herself. To that end, she pushed back her chair to top off her coffee mug. Then she took the few steps across the room to refill Emmett's.

He looked up. "Thank you."

Not one appliance she'd ever been acquainted with had eyes as green as bottle glass. Nor those inky lashes that looked as soft as the matching dark hair on his head. Without thinking, she put out her hand and ran her palm over the tickly, upstanding brush.

He froze.

Too late, she snatched back her hand. Heat burned her face. "Sorry. I'm sorry."

Those lashes dropped over his green eyes. "Don't worry about it." He turned the page of the newspaper, seemingly fascinated by a full-size ad for the grand opening of a quilting store.

"I just wanted to feel your hair," she said, trying to explain the unwarranted action. Her face burned hotter. "I mean, I—"

"Don't worry about it," he said again. Calmly.

At the rehab center, the counselors and therapists very likely told him that sometimes brain-injured people did inappropriate things because their injuries affected their impulse controls. She'd heard about it from her counselors and witnessed it herself among other patients. Before now, she'd never personally shown that particular symptom.

Linda slipped into her seat and slunk low in her chair, willing her embarrassment away. It was no big deal, she told herself. Not when he was a mere helper, like a toaster, like a vending machine.

He was still staring at the quilting-store ad. And she could smell him now, too. Over the scent of the coffee beans she caught that tangy, masculine fragrance that she'd inhaled in the shower. Appliance? Nice try, Linda, but he was all too obviously a man, not a machine.

A man who had willingly given up four weeks of his personal life to live with her.

Why? For the first time, the question blazed to life in her mind. She straightened in her chair.

It should have made her wonder before, she realized, that day at the rehab center. But brain-injured people were often self-centered. As they struggled to recover what skills they could and to learn coping mechanisms for those they'd never regain, their focus was inward, their energy directed toward themselves. That day when he'd volunteered to stay here with her in the guest house, she hadn't really stopped to consider what the situation meant to *him*.

It had to be a sign of the progress she'd made that she was suddenly, unquenchably curious about the man seated across the table from her.

It might even explain her fixation on his scent and her odd compunction to explore the texture of his hair.

"Emmett?"

He grunted; then, when she didn't continue, he looked up.

God, those green eyes were incredible. She almost lost her train of thought. "Why are you here?" she asked.

His eyebrows lifted. "You don't remember?"

She shook her head. "You never said, not really. You mentioned a promise, actually two promises, that you'd made, but not *why* you'd made them."

He took a moment to wrap his hand around his coffee mug and take a deep drink. "Ryan was a not-so-distant relative of mine. We became close during the last few months of his life. When he asked me to do something for him—which meant promising to help *you*—I couldn't say no."

She frowned. There was more, she was sure of it. "Are you from around here?"

He shrugged. "Not really. I've not lived in Texas for a long time. My last permanent address was Sacramento, California. I was assigned to the FBI field office there. But I've been on personal leave from the Bureau for the last several months."

In her long-ago life, she'd been a government agent

herself. It was part of that muzzy past of hers, and another of those jagged-edged pieces that she was trying to integrate into some sort of current identity. But as distant as those memories were, she didn't think an agent taking personal leave for several months was a usual thing. For some reason, she hesitated to voice the question.

"Why would Ryan choose you to make such a promise?" she asked instead. "And why couldn't you say no?"

He waited a beat, staring down into his coffee. Then he looked back up, straight into her eyes. "I don't know why he chose me, but the reason I couldn't say no was because of the hell my brother put him through in those last weeks of his life. The man known as Jason Wilkes, the man who has murdered four people and the man who kidnapped Lily Fortune in February, is my brother."

The bleak expression in his eyes and the raspy note in his voice told her more. Told her more than she wanted to know. It made clear that it was no machine across the table from her. No, she couldn't dismiss him that easily. For the next four weeks, she'd be sharing close quarters with a living, breathing, *feeling* man.

Emmett knew he had to be gentle with Linda, but then he'd gone ahead and put her in startled-doe mode twice during their first morning together. Once, when he'd surprised her in the hall outside the bathroom; the second time, when he'd told her about Jason.

He was still trying to apologize for it later that morning as he drove her to the grocery store. "Look, I'm really sorry about springing that information about my brother on you."

She waved her free hand as she scribbled another item on her grocery list in her lap. "You didn't spring anything on me. I knew about Lily, of course, and have heard mention about the other crimes. I just didn't know of the connection with you."

"I'm sorry," he said again.

"Will you stop that? I'm not some fragile flower, Emmett, that you're duty-bound to shield from the sun and wind. I'm supposed to be getting used to the world, remember?"

But, damn it, he knew the world was full of fragile flowers and the deadly forces out to do them in. The Jessica Chandler case had proved that to him beyond all doubt. The evil done by his brother Jason only underscored it.

Still, Linda could be as stubborn as she was fragile. Once inside the store, she insisted on pushing the cart, her grocery list clutched in one hand. "I can handle this," she told him, wrestling with the cart's wobbly wheels. "Do me a favor and keep your distance."

So he trailed her, never losing sight of her blue jeans and the wave of blond hair that fluttered down her back. She was thin, but with a few more pounds she'd be rounded in all the right places, he decided. And despite her slenderness, her breasts were full. He'd noticed them beneath the transparent cotton of those girlie pajamas she'd been wearing that morning—and then immediately felt guilty for it.

But the young man standing nearby and stocking the breakfast cereal didn't seem to suffer the same pangs of conscience. Emmett watched his bold gaze flick over Linda, checking off face, breasts, legs, then wander back to linger on her chest.

Forgetting her admonition, Emmett strolled up

behind her. "Everything okay, honey?" he asked, shooting a warning look at the cocky kid and placing a hand on Linda's shoulder.

She jumped. "What?"

He soothed her with a gentle stroke of his palm. "Everything okay?"

"I… Sure. What…?" A flush tinged the fair skin of her cheeks.

Emmett smiled when the stock boy took the hint and returned to his work. "The *what* is that pimple-faced Lothario who was leering at you a second ago." Beneath his hand, her arm felt warm and her bones delicate.

Her gaze jumped to the kid, then back to his face. "No," she said. "I'm old enough to be his mother."

He laughed and couldn't stop himself from stroking her arm. "Not a chance." There was nothing the least bit matronly about the soft mouth, the gleaming length of blond hair, those breasts that didn't show much beneath the T-shirt she wore but that he could remember so well from the morning—

He dropped his hand with a silent curse at himself. He was supposed to be Linda's protector, not another lecher like the damn kid up the aisle. "Go on ahead with your shopping."

Another wide-eyed glance, and then she turned away from him to push the cart onward. In the next aisle she paused again, staring at the array of soup cans and sauce jars. Emmett kept his distance, staying several paces behind as she moved on to the bread and rolls, and then the produce section.

It was when she'd lingered there for several frozen minutes that he realized there was nothing in the bottom of the cart. Nothing. Not one item had made it from the shelves into her basket. In that same instant, she started pushing the cart again, moving in rapid strides down the aisle and then out the doors of the store. In her wake, her shopping list fluttered to the blacktop parking lot. He swooped it up, then broke into a jog, catching up with her just as she shoved the cart into a corral of others.

"Linda?"

She whirled, staring at him as if it were the first time she'd seen him. In her wide eyes he saw the unmistakable sheen of tears. Her lower lip trembled.

"Are you all right?" he asked. Stupid question. She wasn't all right. She looked frightened and upset and he didn't know what she needed or how to help her. Without knowing what else to do, he offered her the page of lined paper with its neat column of items. "You dropped this."

Her fingers drew the list from his. "There's so many choices," she whispered, staring down at it. "I wrote *cornflakes,* but there is more than one brand and then so many other kinds of flakes that I couldn't make up my mind which box I wanted. And bread. Wheat bread, white bread, butter-top, multigrain…"

Her voice trailed off as a single tear tracked down her cheek.

She was killing him. Killing him. "It's okay. We'll figure it out." He should have taken her to a smaller store her first time, he thought. A mom-and-pop place where she wouldn't be overwhelmed. "We'll go home now and figure it out later."

"No." Her spine straightened and she lifted her chin, the wet trail of that tear still evident. "No, I can do it."

And damn if she didn't. With that stem of hers stiffened, his fragile flower took herself back into the grocery store. This time he stayed by her side, directing the cart through the aisles and limiting her selections to one or two when she seemed confused or uncertain. They made it back to the car thirty-five minutes later, both of them, he figured, exhausted.

But she still helped load the bags into the back of his truck. Then, as he approached the passenger's door to unlock it for her, he caught sight of her tired, yet elated grin.

"What?" he asked, but he was almost smiling himself, infected by the sense of accomplishment he could see she was feeling. "Pretty proud of yourself, huh?"

She nodded, her grin widening. "Pretty proud of myself, huh. I know it might seem like a small thing to you, but—"

He put his hand over her mouth. "It's no small thing, I know." The warmth of her lips moved against his fingers, and shafts of heat raced across his skin and down his back. He thought of her in those flimsy pajamas again and had to step away.

He looked down at his still-tingling hand. "Did you say something?"

She closed the gap between them. "I said thank-you." And as if it were the most natural thing in the world, Linda Faraday went into his arms.

Technically, he supposed she hugged him, but because his hands closed around her slender back, she was against him, warm and secure within the circle of his body.

It was innocent gratitude on her part, that never-say-die protective instinct on his.

Except that when he breathed in the golden-sunshine

scent of her hair, when he felt her heartbeat through his palms, it was more than protection that rose within him.

It was lust, and it was only going to complicate everything.

Chapter 3

Linda's first day of "independent" living included more dependence than she'd counted upon. But Emmett—the man, not the machine—helped make her first grocery store experience a success. After unloading the food, a light lunch and a much-needed nap, she decided that the morning's accomplishment had given her the courage to take a first step toward tackling the most difficult item on her make-a-life-for-herself list.

It was time for her to try acting like a mother.

She found Emmett in the spare bedroom, tightening the bolts on a treadmill that sat in one corner of the room. He was dressed as she was, in jeans and a T-shirt, though he filled his out much better than her. It took her another moment to look away from him and notice the other pieces of gym equipment in evidence— a pyramid of free weights, three sizes of stability balls, a large, rolled-up mat. "What's all this?" she asked.

"I like to work out," he answered. "You need to. Nancy and Dean agreed to let me outfit this room as a home gym."

"I used to pride myself on my good condition," she remembered, frowning at her reflection in the mirrored closet doors. "Now I'm more stick girl than cover girl."

"You've missed the new trend in cover girls," Emmett replied, leaning one arm against the machine. "For your information, stick is in. But the treadmill is ready to go if you want to give it a whirl."

She shook her head. "Not now. I came to ask another favor of you."

"That's what I'm here for, Linda."

It didn't sit well with her, his promise to Ryan or not. "I'm going to find some way to pay you back."

"Maybe I can think of something myself," he said.

She stilled. There was a deep note in his voice that made her think... But no, he wasn't thinking of her in female terms. Why would he, when she was a woman who couldn't pick out cornflakes without crying first?

"Well, um, until then..." Heat was crawling up her neck and she cursed the silly turn of her thoughts. "I was hoping you could give me a ride to Ricky's school. I thought I'd pick him up today."

"Sure." Emmett straightened and then reached down and stripped off his T-shirt.

Linda stepped back, staring at the broad expanse of male body caught in her gaze. "Wh-what are you doing?"

His eyebrows lifted. "Changing my shirt. I got grease on this one."

"Oh. Well." She couldn't argue with that, nor could she take her eyes off her second up-close-and-personal view of a half-naked man in one day. Now that she thought of it, it was her second up-close-and-personal view of a half-naked man in a decade.

Another flush of heat rushed over her skin, and her breath made a silent whoosh of escape from her lungs. The fact was, she hadn't been thinking of herself in female terms, but now it seemed as if her freedom from the rehab facility had freed something else—the knowledge that the past ten years hadn't damaged her hormones.

Emmett paused beside her on his way out of the room. "Do you feel okay?"

His skin was golden and smooth, and the route from his muscled shoulder to the bulge of his rock-hard bicep was fascinating. She swallowed. "I, um, I'm fine."

He reached out a finger and tapped her nose in a big-brotherly gesture. "Give me two minutes and then we'll go."

She spent the two minutes telling herself it was perfectly normal to have sexual feelings. It was a good thing. Another sign of progress, another optimistic portent that she could be a complete person at some future date, that she could be a whole woman—which would include, most importantly, being a mother.

Mother.

Just thinking the word caused her hormones to evaporate and everything else inside of her to freeze up. But she managed to follow Emmett to the car and tried to appear composed as he pulled into a parking spot near the school.

Linda checked her watch, licked her dry lips. "We're early."

Unrolling the windows with the electronic controls, Emmett shrugged. "No problem. We'll wait."

But waiting made her nervous. To distract herself,

she scanned the cars nearby, checking out the other mothers waiting behind their wheels. They all seemed to be doing three things at once—talking on cell phones and filing their nails and scanning small calendars, or talking on cell phones, sipping bottled water and handing toys to small children in car seats. They wore their hair in perky short cuts or high perky ponytails.

She combed her fingers through her long, straight fall of blond hair. "Maybe I should do something with all this."

"It's beautiful."

Her chin jerked toward Emmett. She'd forgotten he was there. "What?"

"Your hair. It's beautiful. You're beautiful."

She felt herself flushing again. "You…I…I wasn't fishing for compliments."

"I'm stating facts. I saw how you were looking at the other women and it wasn't so hard to follow your train of thought. You don't need to worry about how you measure up."

"You're quite the observer," she said, not sure that she liked that about him.

He shrugged. "Just some of Uncle Sam's fine training. But you're familiar with that, aren't you? Ryan said you were an agent with the Treasury Department before your accident. That you were looking into some discrepancies in the books at Fortune TX, Ltd. and that's how you met Cameron Fortune, Ricky's father."

"Cameron Fortune." She repeated the name, then looked away. "I'll bet your Uncle Sam training made it clear you shouldn't get personal with the target of an investigation. That you shouldn't fall in love with him and then do something as stupid as sleep with him."

"Is that what happened?" Emmett asked quietly.

"I don't know." She scrubbed her hands over her face. "That's what Ryan pieced together in the days after the accident. But when I came fully conscious, I couldn't add any more to the story. My memory of those months at the Fortunes' company are completely gone. I remember crossing the stage to receive my master's degree when I was twenty-one years old. I remember going straight from there to the fifteen-week new-agent training course. The next thing I remember is Nancy Armstrong talking to me, her face starting to sharpen in focus. I looked her straight in the eye and told her I wanted a Diet Pepsi, the first clear words I'd spoken in nine years. But between the diploma and the diet drink…almost nothing."

"Nothing of your feelings for Cameron?"

Lifting her hands, she shook her head. "No."

"Must make it hard to believe you're a mother, then."

She was afraid to admit to it. "But I am. Ricky's been blessed to have Nancy and Dean. They've raised him as their grandson. But I'm his mother." *And, please, God, let me start feeling like one any moment now.* She cared about the little boy. It wasn't hard to enjoy a rambunctious, normal kid, but *mothering* him… How did one learn the rules of that?

In the distance, a school bell rang. Around them, car doors opened and those confident, perky-haired mothers emerged, cell phones still in one hand, satchel-size purses or bottles of water or toddlers in the other.

Taking a deep breath, Linda pushed down on the door handle. "I'll be right back," she told Emmett.

"I'll come with you."

A real mother wouldn't need his presence, but she didn't bother putting up even a token protest. Instead, she shoved her hands into the front pockets of her jeans and followed the trail of women heading toward the front gates of the school.

A troop of kids in yellow plastic hard hats emerged first, some carrying Stop signs. Linda glanced over at Emmett.

"Traffic patrol," he said.

The traffic patrol! Of course it was the traffic patrol—the older kids of the elementary school who were charged with getting the littler ones safely across the street. As she watched, individuals peeled off the small crew to stake out the corners of the nearby intersection while more little kids poured out of the gates. Some headed for yellow school buses, some ran into the arms of the cell phone mothers, and groups gathered to cross the streets.

In the streaming parade of children emerging from the school, Linda couldn't find Ricky.

Studying the faces around her, she made her way toward those open front gates, her shins bumped by plastic lunch boxes, her thighs thumped by backpacks that gave each little kid linebacker shoulders. "Ricky!" she heard a high voice yell, and she spun left to follow the sound, but lost the speaker in a sea of pigtails and porcupine-spiked hair.

She whirled back, telling herself she'd find her son, telling herself not to panic, telling herself even a person without a brain injury might be confused within the mass of chattering voices and afternoon exuberance. *Breathe, Linda, breathe.*

"Grrrr!" Something knee-high and wearing a gruesome, paper-plate-with-poster-paint mask came at her, eyes glittering, bitty fingers curled into claws. Linda drew instinctively away from it, and her back hit someone else's solid frame.

Emmett's. He held her against him with an arm across her waist. "It's a jungle out here, isn't it?" he said against his ear.

Even as his warm breath sent goose bumps sprinting down her neck, Linda relaxed against him. Just as it had in the grocery store, his presence calmed her and gave her renewed strength.

"I don't see Ricky," she said. "Could we have missed him?" The cell phone moms hadn't missed their kids. Already they were climbing back into their cars, their kids in tow, their mouths still moving as they continued their calls.

"We didn't miss him." Emmett placed a hand atop each of her shoulders and turned her back to the intersection of streets. "See that Stop sign over there?"

Attached to the Stop sign was Ricky, his features almost lost beneath the plastic yellow brim of his hard hat. Her son, Ricky. Star of the traffic patrol.

At least, that was how it seemed to her. A swell of warmth rose inside her as she watched him nod to the group of children waiting on his corner. They hurried through the crosswalk under his serious gaze.

She looked up at Emmett. "He's very good at that, don't you think?"

"Truly a prodigy."

Her eyes narrowed. "Are you laughing at me?"

He shook his head. "No. You just sounded so motherish."

She considered the notion. "No, I don't have the cell phone for it."

"What?"

"Never mind." She returned her gaze to Ricky, watching as he monitored the last of the crossers, then tucked his Stop sign under his arm and headed back for the school. She realized the instant he saw her.

"Hi," she said, hoping she still had that motherish tone that Emmett had noted. Maybe if she sounded like a mother and acted the part, she'd really begin to feel like one. "Good day at school?"

"What are you doing here?" he asked, his eyes darting toward his patrol buddies and then back to her face.

"I thought maybe you'd like a ride home today, instead of taking the school bus. We could stop for… ice cream or something." She glanced up for Emmett's approval, but he'd drifted away from her and Ricky.

"I want to take the bus." His glance flicked over to another boy, who was standing shoulder to shoulder with him. "Anthony and I always take the bus home together."

She shrugged. "We could take Anthony with us. For the ice cream, too."

Anthony's dark-chocolate eyes widened. "I can't go home with a stranger. My mother would kill me!"

"I'm not a stranger," Linda started to say, but Ricky was pushing his friend toward the school.

"C'mon, Anthony, we have to put our signs and stuff away," he said, herding the other boy off.

"Ricky, wait!"

He turned back reluctantly. "What do you want now?"

"I—" She sighed. "You really want to go home on the bus?"

"Yeah."

She rubbed her palms against the front of her jeans. "Well, then, I guess that's what you should do. I apologize for coming here without checking with you first.

And I apologize about thinking I could take Anthony with us. I didn't think. I didn't realize—"

"That he'd get in trouble. A real mom would know that." He turned and walked away from her.

A real mom would know that. A real mom.

She couldn't fool Ricky, could she? Even if she sounded like a mom, acted like a mom, learned all the mom rules, none of those would get her anywhere if Ricky himself didn't want the mother in his life to be her.

Emmett didn't need the skills of observation he'd honed through his FBI experience to know that Linda's conversation with Ricky hadn't gone well. Not only had she walked away without the boy, she'd spent the entire ride back home in a deep silence.

He'd let her stew, because he didn't know what else she needed.

Back at the guest house, when she asked him to show her how to use the new treadmill, he'd hoped the exercise would exorcise the demons that were plaguing her.

Instead, they seemed to be punishing her.

She'd already been on the machine for thirty minutes, her speed increasing from a walk to a fast walk to a brisk jog, as if she were trying to outrun whatever was bothering her. The shorts and T-shirt she'd changed into clung to her perspiring body and the tendrils of hair around her face were wet.

Still, she kept on moving, her long ponytail swishing behind her back, her running shoes slap-slap-slapping against the treadmill's belt.

Under the pretext of doing his own workout, he'd kept an eye on her. But he couldn't pretend any longer that he wasn't worried.

"Maybe you should quit," he called from across the room over the machine's hum.

She acted as if she didn't hear him, so he set down the free weights he'd been pumping and strolled over to her. He stood right in front of the piece of equipment, ducking his head a little so that their gazes met. "Maybe you should quit," he repeated.

"Believe me...I'm thinking...about it," she panted out.

"Quit running," he clarified, then leaned forward to reach the keypad where he could reduce the speed of the belt. "It's time for your cooldown."

She frowned at him, though her feet slowed. "Don't need...a keeper," she got out. "Used to be...fit. Very fit."

"You'll be fit again." He punched the pad a second time, reducing the speed even more. "Unless you give yourself a heart attack first. And I charge extra for CPR."

She made a face at him, even as she sucked in a couple of long breaths. "You don't believe me... Used to be one tough woman."

Her pace had slowed to a walk, and he let his gaze linger on her slim legs and their long stride. Toughness wasn't an antidote to evil and tragedy, he thought to himself, frowning. Ryan had been tough. Lily Fortune was tough. But they hadn't escaped the darkness the world could deal out. Jessica Chandler had been tough, too—the sweetest, toughest victim he'd ever tried to help—but in the end she'd been just that—a victim.

"Secret agent accountant."

That brought his attention back to the present. "What did you say?"

Walking with her hands on her hips, she took another deep breath. "That's how I saw myself. Sure, I had degrees in the dry fields of finance and business, but when I was recruited as an agent for the Treasury Department, I saw myself as Linda Faraday, secret agent accountant."

It made his lips quirk. "You *were* young, weren't you?" he murmured.

"Our new-agent course included firearms as well as physical training. Not as intense as what you G-men go through, but I thought I could handle myself."

Her fingers touched the keypad, and the treadmill's hum stopped. Linda stepped off the machine and grabbed the small towel hanging on its handrails. She blotted her face with it, her words coming out muffled. "Apparently it wasn't *physical* training that I needed, but emotional."

She was talking about her affair, her affair with the subject of an investigation—Cameron Fortune. Sudden anger snapped inside Emmett, surprising him with its stinging lash. Ryan's brother had been twice her age and canny, no doubt. *The son of a bitch,* Emmett thought. *The son of a bitch took advantage of Linda and then irrevocably changed her life.*

But Emmett kept his emotions off his face and out of his voice. "He was a handsome and charming man, by all reports."

She looked at him over the towel, strangling it between her hands. "That's supposed to make me feel better?" she asked, her voice bitter. "The person I thought I was wouldn't be swayed by good looks and charm."

Though he was lousy at light banter, he tried to ease the tension of the moment. "Oh, good. Then maybe I have a chance with you."

She didn't crack a smile. "As if I would know what to do if I had you. I was no good as Linda Faraday, secret agent accountant. Ricky doesn't think anything of me as a mother. I doubt I'm much of a woman, either."

Despite those words, her flowery, female scent was in the air, tickling his nose, shaking awake the lust that he'd felt when he'd held her in his arms that morning. He couldn't stop himself from pushing back a damp tendril of her bright hair. "Give yourself time."

"I *can't,* don't you see? I've lost so much time already. In another ten years, Ricky won't need a mother."

What could he say to that? What could he do to help? Unfortunately for Linda, he wasn't the pep-talk type. His true expertise lay in looking at the dark side of life. "What's the alternative?" he asked.

She spun away. "Giving up."

The two words froze him. Not because he didn't understand the impulse, but because he'd done it himself. After the Jessica Chandler case, so closely following his brother Chris's murder, he'd given up and run away to the cabin in the Sandias. If he had his way, he'd probably still be there. Still be half-drunk. Still be full of pain.

Now he was sober. And still full of pain.

Linda spun back. "But I *can't.* I won't. I have a responsibility to Ricky, an obligation to Nancy and Dean who never gave up on me. Do you see?"

"I do." It was the truth. "Sometimes what keeps us going is not what we want, but what we owe to other people."

She studied his face. "The promise you made to Ryan."

"And to myself. To my parents. To the memory of my brother Christopher."

Linda winced. "I'm sorry." She touched a hand to her forehead, then laid her fingers on his arm. "The injury… I'm still working on not thinking everything revolves around me, me, me. I'm complaining, but you're in a bad place, too, and yet you're here, playing Mary Poppins to me."

He raised his eyebrows. "As long as you don't ask me to fly you around with my umbrella."

Her fingers tightened on him and her touch was once again warming his blood, that lust distracting him. "Seriously, Emmett. I know I'm not quite a whole person, let alone a sounding board, but I'm here if you want to talk."

"I'm not much of a talker. I was always the lone wolf in the family."

"You're in luck," she said with a half smile. "I practiced my silence for many years."

Then she showed him how good she was at it. She sat down on the edge of the treadmill's ramp, then patted the spot beside her. He surprised himself by obeying, seating himself next to her while the quiet grew around them.

She crossed her arms on top of her bent knees and rested her cheek there. He gazed at the back of her head while listening to the sounds of spring outside. Birds were trilling, peeping, cheeping. A branch, jostled by the warm wind, scratched against the glass of the window. Dogs barked in the distance.

A sense of the season settled over him. Springtime. Renewal. Hope.

Linda's eyes were closed and he wondered if she was

asleep. Her lashes were dark brown and curled against the soft pink of her cheeks.

"You're still a woman, you know," he murmured.

She wasn't asleep, at least not all the way. Her lashes rose and she sat up, slanting him a half-drowsy glance. "You think?"

"I know." Their gazes held. Darker pink color tinged her fair skin. His hand reached out and he palmed her warm cheek. "Shall I prove it to you?"

She swallowed. "Not because you're obligated."

He shook his head. "Not because I'm obligated." But because he didn't like to see her sad. Because he thought he could take one worry off her mind. Oh, yeah, and then there was that lust. He'd known it would complicate things, but right now he didn't care.

Leaning close, he touched his lips to hers.

She jerked against his hand, as if he'd stung her, but he'd been gentle. He was gentle. So, so gentle.

For a moment, she kissed like a child might, her mouth pursed and stiff, but then she softened. Her lips parted, but he didn't pretend it was an intimate invitation. Instead, he let her warm up to the kiss, let her warm up to him, without doing any more than keeping his mouth pressed close to hers.

"You should breathe," he whispered against her mouth. "You still need air."

"Is that why I see stars?"

It made him smile, and he drew back to look at her.

She traced his lips with two fingers. "You don't do that often enough. Smile, I mean."

"Keep kissing me and maybe I will."

But she was shaking her head. "I have your number, you know. I'm getting smarter by the minute when it comes to you."

"How's that?"

She straightened away from him. "You're sweet."

He stared at her. "Sweet? You're kidding, right?"

"You're sweet."

"I'm cynical. Cold. Distant. Determined. Ask anyone."

Shaking her head, she rose to her feet. "I don't need to. I was feeling low and not very confident and you kissed me. That's sweet."

"I didn't do it to be sweet!"

She had the wide blue eyes of a baby. "Then why did you?"

"Because…" It had nothing to do with sweetness. It was because he thought she was beautiful and sexy, which, if she wasn't so sweet herself, she'd see proof of in the tight fit of his now uncomfortable jeans.

"Told you." With a little grin, she spun on one foot and sauntered out, her hips swishing with a sassy little twitch.

That womanly touch was almost worth being called sweet. Almost.

"Don't fool yourself," he called after her. "I'm cynical. Cold. Distant. Determined. Just wait and I'll prove it to you."

The bathroom door closing was her answer.

He was still smiling—smiling again!—when his cell phone rang. It sat on a low table he'd pushed to the side of the room, so he made a long reach for it.

"Jamison here."

"And here, too," a voice said.

Emmett forgot about spring and sunshine. Darkness closed in on him again. He felt it, smelled it, sensed the sulfur whiff of evil in the air. Striding to the doorway of the exercise room, he glanced down the hall to keep watch on the bathroom door. To make sure Linda was safe.

"Where the hell are you, Jason?"

"Do you think I called to tell you, little brother? Then you're stupider than I thought."

Emmett gritted his teeth at his brother's taunting. In a perverse sense, Jason was entitled to his arrogance. The police had had him in custody once and then he'd escaped to kidnap Lily Fortune. Later, even with experienced men like Emmett in the mix, the FBI had lost him during the ransom exchange. And an agent had lost his life.

"We figured you'd be on your way to the South Pacific or South America with the ransom money by now," Emmett said, calming his voice.

"You'd like me out of the country, wouldn't you?"

What Emmett would like was to find his brother and stop him once and for all. It was what he'd vowed to do. Cynical, cold, distant, determined. If Linda could look inside him right now, she'd have no doubt about the kind of man he was.

"I'd like to know why you called, Jason."

"I read this morning's Red Rock newspaper."

There was a clue. His brother was near enough to Red Rock to have easy access to the local paper. What it might have said, though, Emmett had no idea. Since he was in San Antonio now, he read the San Antonio paper. But Jason couldn't know what city he was in and Emmett certainly wasn't about to tell him. His brother was smart enough without providing him any aid. "I didn't get a chance to read it yet myself."

"Didn't get a chance to read it," Jason mocked, his voice rising. "You don't need to read it to know that Ryan Fortune left you a bundle of cash and stock options."

Apparently some of the details of Ryan's will had been leaked to the press. It might have irritated Emmett if it hadn't also brought Jason out of the woodwork. "Hey, it wasn't my choice, Jase. That was Ryan's doing."

"Why should you get any of the Fortune money when it was me who worked so hard for it?"

Jason had thought himself entitled to the Fortune wealth since they were kids, and their grandfather, Farley Jamison, had been obsessed with the money as a means to fund his grandiose political aspirations. "But you have some of the Fortune money—Lily's ransom," Emmett pointed out.

"I don't care about that," Jason snapped.

Emmett frowned. "You don't care about the money?"

"Not as much as I care about taking *you* down, little brother. Keep looking over your shoulder, Emmett, because I'm coming after you. Then I'll have my reward. And my revenge."

The call clicked off. Emmett remained standing, staring at the phone in his hand. Well, well, well. This put a new spin on things.

The man Emmett had promised himself to stop had just promised to stop *him*.

Fine, he thought.

May the best man win.

Chapter 4

Emmett sat at the kitchen table the next morning, the last of a pot of coffee now a final swallow in the bottom of his mug. The dregs of black liquid were as dark as his mood after a sleepless night going over Jason's phone call.

I'm coming after you, his brother had said.

As if Emmett were like the proverbial sitting duck, waiting for his brother to take him out.

He wasn't afraid of Jason. But there was no doubt the other man was wily and Emmett had others to think of besides himself. However, Jason didn't have a clue as to where Emmett was residing at the moment and would never think to look for him in the Armstrong's guest house. Jason didn't know that the older couple or Ricky and Linda even existed, so Emmett was reasonably sure they were safe from Jason's latest threat.

But damn, the truth was Emmett was just sitting around.

Taking care of this promise regarding Linda meant he wasn't taking care of the problem that was Jason. It put the ball in his brother's court—*I'm coming after you*—and Emmett didn't like it. At all. He was used to controlling the action, not letting others control *him*.

"G'morning."

His gaze lifted in time to see a sleepy-eyed Linda enter the room. She was wearing a thick robe and terry-cloth slippers, had bedhead and a pillowcase crease across her left cheek.

He grunted, tightening his grip on his coffee mug as desire pinballed through his system. For some inconvenient reason, she gave him a bad case of the gimmes.

She squinched her eyes at him and pushed back a hank of her iron-straight, golden hair. "You *are* Emmett Jamison, yes?"

Was this another symptom of her brain injury? Had she forgotten him, or was she joking around? "The last I checked, that's me."

She nodded. "Good. I thought so, but the way you greeted me set me off my stride for a second."

"The way I greeted you?"

"That cheerful good morning grunt."

"Oh." She was joking around. "Sorry."

Her hand waved. "No apology necessary. I'm not much of a morning person myself. It's just that after I came out of my…condition, I found myself often confused by new and unfamiliar faces. So I learned to gauge whether I was already acquainted with someone by the warmth of their response to me. Yours was a sort of stranger-type grunt."

Funny, how she could make him half grin and feel guilty at the same time. Then more guilty when he saw that she was staring at the now-empty coffeepot. "Let me," he said, starting to rise.

"No, no, no." She waved him down again. "I can do this. I can make coffee. We had a practice kitchen in rehab. Like kindergarten class, you know? We played house in order to relearn how to do simple tasks."

He watched her trudge to the counter. She pulled close the bean grinder he'd left on the tiled surface and lifted off the clear plastic top to reveal plenty of freshly ground beans. Then she removed the basket from the coffeemaker. Inside was the used filter and a mess of wet grounds.

She stared at them. Then her gaze moved to the grinder. Back to the full basket.

Like yesterday in the grocery store, he could feel the confusion radiate off her slim body. Her spine became as straight as a steel rod, and her shoulders looked stiff. Something in the middle of his chest hurt.

He was almost out of his chair when she spoke, her voice tight. "Remind me again. What should I do?"

Breath he hadn't realized he'd been holding slid out of him in a silent whoosh. "Throw the old grounds and filter into the wastebasket under the sink," he said, careful to keep his voice free of anything but information. "We put the fresh filters in that clear jar over there by the grinder."

She crossed to the sink and he watched her reach for the wastebasket even as he pretended not to. He held his breath again and caught himself—barely—before telling her not to throw out the plastic basket along with the old filter and beans.

She caught herself—barely—before doing just that. Emmett let out a silent cheer as she rinsed the basket and then crossed back to the coffeemaker. "I knew that," she said conversationally as she fitted in a clean filter. "That part about throwing away the used filter and grounds. But we'd only practiced with a clean coffeemaker in rehab and little things like that can stump me. I know there's something I should do, and if it was on a multiple-choice test, I would recognize the answer. But sometimes I can't dredge up the information from wherever it's sleeping in my consciousness."

His chest was hurting again and he said the first thing that came into his head. "I admire you for being able to ask for help. That can't be easy."

"It isn't easy." She finished preparing the coffee, then set the switch to On. "I don't want to need help. I don't want to admit I need help almost as much. But it's a fact of life until I get more practice."

She moved to the oven and set the timer, then turned to meet his gaze. "Strategies. Props. That's how I get by. One of my strategies is to set a timer to remind myself to stay on task. Five minutes for coffee. When it goes off, I'll check the maker. Without the alarm I might sit here for a while and never remember what I'm waiting for. Unless I write it down in my notebook— another of my favorite props."

Her matter-of-factness was just something else to admire. No whining, no play for pity. The counselors at her rehab facility had told him about Linda's strategies and props in order to prepare him for helping her out—and they'd also let him know that she was well on her way to needing them less and less—but they hadn't prepared him for how watching her use them would leave him feeling so…

There weren't words for it.

So, ignoring that ache in his chest, he grunted again and pulled a section of the San Antonio paper in front of him. He didn't look up until the kitchen alarm went off and she was back at the table after filling up his mug and then her own.

"Thank you," he said.

"That's my line," Linda replied. "I don't think I was that good at being grateful pre traumatic brain injury, but it seems to be another skill I'm slowly learning to acquire."

"You don't—"

"I am, Emmett. Grateful and beholden. To the Armstrongs. To you. I don't know how I'll ever repay any of you."

"Linda—"

"Don't tell me I'm wrong. My brain isn't that dead."

"Wait a sec—"

"Oh, come on."

"But—"

"Emmett, what could you possibly get out of this situation?"

"Lessons in how to edge a word into the conversation when sharing the breakfast table with a woman?"

Her velvety blue eyes rounded over the rim of her coffee mug. Then she laughed. "Okay. Apologies next."

"Those are unnecessary, too."

"Well, I'm certain you don't need practice facing women across a breakfast table."

"What about across a kitchen table?" He leaned back in his chair to study her. "Outside of my mother, you might be my first, come to think of it."

Her eyes registered surprise again. "No wife? No ex?"

"Never married."

"Fiancée?"

He shook his head.

"No lovers?" she asked, her eyes rounding even more.

"Of course I've had lovers!" Maybe she was joking around again, but he discovered his ego couldn't take the chance.

"Ah." That little smile playing around her mouth told him she had been joking after all. "But no long-term lovers. Nobody you wanted to share a bathroom or a breakfast with."

"I'm a pretty solitary guy. Have been my whole life."

She nodded. "How old are you?"

"Thirty-one."

"Hah," she said, that little smile reclaiming her pretty lips. She put one elbow on the table and leaned toward him. "I'm older than you. Maybe you *can* learn something from me."

Such as how to control the lust that was rising in him like steam off the coffee in their mugs. The movement she'd made had opened a gap between the lapels of her nubby-textured robe. It exposed an expanse of pale skin and the fragile structure of her collarbone.

He'd always been a protector—it had been the lure of the FBI—and it was something he'd accepted about himself years ago. So Linda should be just another victim to him, just another one of those he was driven to keep safe. But he'd never felt this…pull toward anyone he'd rescued, or anyone he was charged with keeping secure. Not even Jessica Chandler and her family.

He was going to shut it down, right now, because it was unnecessary and distracting, and had nothing to do with the promises he'd made.

Take care of Linda and Ricky.

Put a stop to Jason.

The woman was still smiling at him from across the

table. He could smell her, damn it, the same scent that drove him crazy in every room she'd been in. It was flowers and sunshine and a freshness that he would only bruise and darken with his big hands, foul moods and ugly family history.

Shoving back his chair, he stood.

She stood, too. "Emmett?" she asked, a frown between her brows.

See? He was already marking her, marring her, taking away her smiles.

He was better off alone. Ryan should have extracted the promise to care for Linda from someone else.

"Emmett?" Linda asked again.

He ran a hand over his hair. "My brother..." Tell her, he urged himself. Tell her that his vow to find his brother superseded everything. It was what he should do, because it would be safer for all of them. Leave this house and go on the hunt for Jason. Linda would find someone else, someone kinder, more lighthearted, less lustful, to help her make coffee and to shop for groceries and to ease the ache of not connecting with her child.

She put her hand on his arm. "Are you worrying about him? I heard you moving around last night. Is Jason the reason you couldn't sleep?"

Emmett stared down at the pale, slender fingers resting against the darker skin of his forearm. He'd hated the feeling that Jason was controlling him. But now... Now he was at Linda's mercy, too. There was no denying it.

He wanted to be the one for her. For right now, anyway. Until she was better prepared for her new life. Just until then.

He found himself covering her hand with his free

one. He couldn't help himself. "I don't want to think of my brother at all," he said, realizing that was true, as well. "I just want to kiss you."

And without her permission, his head bent toward hers. Without her permission, he sank into another kiss.

And didn't mind the loss of control at all.

Holding a cheap disposable razor, Jason Jamison, aka Jason Wilkes, smiled at his reflection in the cracked mirror over the cracked bathroom sink in the crappy motel in a crappy small town not all that far from Red Rock. While he was accustomed to better surroundings, the knowledge that his little brother Emmett was certain to be shaking in his boots and stewing over Jason's whereabouts this morning was too damn good not to savor.

A loner and a loser, that was his brother Emmett. A sanctimonious do-gooder who had never possessed the true Jamison vision. His other brother, Christopher, hadn't, either. Jason had hated that Boy Scout Christopher since they were kids and mainly ignored the younger Emmett. But now that Chris was finally out of his hair—thanks to Jason's decisive, fatal action when St. Christopher had tried to talk him about of his plan of revenge against the Fortunes—asshole Emmett was now in his sights.

And Jason was a damn good shot.

Handling guns was one of the things he'd been taught by his grandfather, Farley Jamison.

The other was how the Fortune family had cheated Farley, and thus Jason himself, out of a powerful place in politics. Years before, Kingston Fortune, Farley's half brother, had refused to bankroll Farley's entrée into the Texas political scene. Jason's grandfather had never recovered from the disappointment and after his death, it had been up to Jason to avenge Farley's broken dreams by finding a way to topple Kingston's empire, which had been run by Ryan Fortune until his recent death.

Jason scraped the razor through the layer of shaving cream on his cheek. Though plastic surgery after an accident in his early twenties meant he no longer possessed the Jamison features, he didn't mind. His father and his brothers were weak men who didn't have the talent or ruthlessness to get what Jason had.

Two million dollars. A fake passport. Stolen credit cards. Everything a guy would need to get out of Texas and start a new life, knowing that he'd left a swathe of destruction in his wake. He'd scared the crap out of Ryan Fortune during the last few months of his life, even as the man was dying of a brain tumor, by kidnapping his beloved Lily.

That was what the old fool got for loving anyone better than himself.

Jason had never made that mistake. It was why it hadn't been so hard to kill his two-timing bitch of a girlfriend. Melissa had started it, anyway, striking out at him with her fists and her words. When she'd said he was going to end up as big a loser as his grandfather Farley, Jason had shut her up with his two hands around her skinny, trailer-trash throat. He was glad, damn glad, that she wasn't around to reap the benefits of his brilliance.

All the impediments to his future were out of the way now. He could ride off into the proverbial sunset with his saddlebags full of Fortune cash and have himself a hell of a good life.

As soon as he got rid of Emmett.

It wasn't part of his original plan, but then, a brilliant man had to be flexible. And decisive.

Emmett annoyed him, so Emmett had to die. Jason wasn't leaving Texas until he'd taken care of that one last task.

Today is Monday.
You have lunch with Nancy in the main house at noon.
Avoid Emmett. He practically kissed you into another coma two mornings ago.
You don't want Nancy to know how much you're still struggling with your brain injury.

Linda glanced at her open notebook one last time and then shut its tagboard cover. With a deep breath, she exited her bedroom and hurried for the guest cottage's front door. She heard the rhythmic *phizz-wizz, phizz-wizz* of the rowing machine mechanism coming from the workout room and was glad she could pinpoint Emmett's exact location. She couldn't take another surprise from him and still keep her composure in front of Nancy. Nan, she corrected herself, using the abbreviation that Ricky had coined. The shortened name had stuck.

Linda wanted Nan to see her at her best and getting better.

The Armstrongs' cook let her in the back door and then guided her through the kitchen to where Nancy was waiting for her in the small parlor. Before a wide window looking out into the garden, a tea cart was set with two places. Nan herself was waiting for Linda on a floral couch angled in a corner of the sunny room.

"There you are!" The older woman beamed at Linda and rose to her feet to embrace her.

"Am I late?" Linda kissed her cheek and then sat against the cushions.

"No, no. I'm just anxious to hear how you're settling in."

"Wonderful. Great. Perfect. The guest house is so comfortable and charming. So convenient and cozy." Linda silenced herself before she babbled another wave of adjectives. Too many sounded insincere, she reminded herself. Worse, too many sounded as if she belonged back in rehab.

After all the Armstrongs had done for her and for Ricky, she couldn't fail in her bid to make herself a new life.

"And Emmett?" Nan asked. "How are the two of you getting along?"

"Emmett?" At the sound of his name, a vision of him popped into Linda's head. He'd looked dark and sleek when she'd stumbled, sleep stupored, into the kitchen two mornings ago. His still-damp hair had been brushed back from his forehead and he'd been wearing that dark, forbidding expression that appeared to be his habit. But she'd made him smile, and later...later...

"Linda?"

She started, her gaze jumping back to Nan's face. "What?"

"I asked about Emmett and you seemed to lose your train of thought."

Linda felt the heat of embarrassment climb her cheeks. The train had been about to travel into dangerous, distracting territory. Another lingering symptom of brain injury was that her concentration could easily wander. "Emmett's fine," she said, focusing on Nan's gentle blue eyes. "He took me grocery shopping on Friday and then to meet Ricky after school."

"I heard about that," Nan said, reaching out to pat Linda's forearm. "I told your son he should have let you give him a ride home."

Your son. Her son. Ricky. She had to get better for him. She had to learn how to be a strong, whole person because her son was her responsibility.

If not her love.

That traitorous thought whispered through her brain, and she couldn't squelch it. Loving Ricky would come in time, just as relearning to make coffee, relearning to drive and all the other things she had to do would come back, now that she was awake and out of rehab.

They would all come back…wouldn't they? Tears stung the corners of her eyes and she looked away to hide them from the older woman.

"Linda, dear—"

Whatever Nancy was about to say was interrupted by the cook, who entered the room carrying a tray with two steaming soup bowls. It gave Linda time to gather her composure. Eating the delicious chicken tortilla soup gave her a boost of optimism that only home-made soup could provide.

Several spoonfuls later, she smiled across the table at Nancy. "And how have you been? Isn't tomorrow your bridge day?"

"No, that's Wednesday. Tomorrow's Tuesday, when I volunteer in Ricky's classroom." Nan looked down at her bowl, hesitated. "Would you…"

No. She was going to ask Linda to accompany her. She was going to ask Linda to play mother at Ricky's school. Hadn't she already failed at that on Friday?

Change the subject, avoid the request, she thought in desperation. "What do you know about Emmett?"

"Emmett?"

Once again, his name sent Linda's mind on another detour. Emmett had kissed her in the kitchen. It was another kindness, a comfort, some human-to-human contact. That was all. But it felt like so much more to her. His hard mouth against hers had sent prickles at a run over her chin and down her neck. Prickles that tightened her nipples, that then turned to tingles that slid down and between her thighs.

Her knees had gone as soft as her head.

Then she'd experienced what they called in rehab a "flood," when she found herself awash in her emotions. And just thinking about that kiss made her experience it all over again—her thoughts, her actions, her language skills overwhelmed by the temptation and tenderness in that one, simple, lip-to-lip lock.

"Linda?"

She jerked her gaze to Nan's once again. *Cover, cover, cover,* she reminded herself. *Don't let her see how far from whole you still are.*

Marshaling her wits and her composure, she pasted on a smile. "Sorry. As I was saying, what do you know about—" *Not Emmett again!* "—Emmett's brother. Emmett's brother Jason."

"Jason." Nan frowned. "Why are you asking about him?"

Because he seems like a safe enough topic. Certainly safer than Ricky or Emmett himself. "He came up in conversation with Emmett. I recall he was the one who kidnapped Lily a few months ago, but I'm not clear on any other details about him."

Nan shook her head. "It's one of those sad stories

that defy explanation. How can one son turn out so bad, how can one man create such havoc?"

"He did more than kidnap Lily? That I remember, of course, but Emmett said he's also murdered some others. And that Ryan is a distant relative. Is that why Lily was targeted?"

"The connection between the Jamisons and the Fortunes is one of those sagas that more than one family could probably find hiding along with the skeletons in their closets. Ryan told Dean and me about it before his death, and apparently it's a story that Jason Jamison knew as well—and then twisted in his mind to become the motivation for his crimes."

"What exactly *is* the connection between the Jamisons and the Fortunes?"

"It's a *who*," Nan replied. "Kingston Fortune, Ryan's father."

And Ricky's grandfather, Linda thought. Cameron, Ricky's father, had been Ryan's older brother and so would have been another of Kingston Fortune's sons. "Go on," she said.

"In Iowa in the early 1900s, a handsome son of a wealthy family, Travis Jamison, got a young farm girl pregnant. He was shipped out of state before he knew about the child, and its unwed, disgraced mother left the baby boy with a family in the next county—the Fortunes, who named him Kingston. It was he who built the Fortune empire here in San Antonio and in the Red Rock area."

"So who put the Jamisons and the Fortunes in touch with each other again?"

"Travis Jamison's sister discovered the connection. Travis married, had two sons and then died in the 1930s. But Aunt Bonnie doted on Travis's sons, Joseph and Farley. Farley went to law school and then into politics. He married and had three children, none who truly inherited his same itch for power. He lost an important election, and it was then that Aunt Bonnie told him about a long-lost relative she'd found—Kingston Fortune. He was Farley's half brother, wealthy and influential enough to buy Farley a powerful political office in Texas."

Linda's soup bowl was empty. She reached for the basket of crusty rolls. A story like this one was good for her appetite. "Did Kingston help Farley?"

Nan shook her head. "He wouldn't even meet with him. The more uncooperative Kingston was, the more Farley became obsessed with him. He ultimately ended up in a run-down cabin outside of Houston, where he would rant and rave about the Texas Fortunes to anyone who would listen, particularly one of his grandsons."

"Jason."

"That's right. Farley's son Blake had three boys, Christopher, Jason and Emmett. Christopher was a teacher—"

"And Emmett an FBI agent."

"And Jason..." Nan shrugged. "In my youth, we called a boy like that one a bad seed."

"What did he want from the Fortunes?"

Nan shrugged again. "The papers speculate that he started out wanting to ruin Ryan Fortune's businesses as retribution for the help never given to Farley. Who knows? The fact is, his older brother, Christopher, tracked Jason here to Texas last year hoping to steer him away from his dangerous interest in the Fortunes. But Jason killed Christopher."

Linda gasped. "One of the people he murdered was his own brother?"

"That's right. He dumped the body in Lake Mondo, but when it was recovered it was found to have a birthmark on the back right hip—a birthmark distinctive to the Fortunes of Texas."

"Does Ricky?"

Nan nodded. "Ricky has it, too. When the body from the lake was ultimately identified as Christopher Jamison, it was his father, Blake Jamison, who told Ryan of the circumstances of Kingston Fortune's birth. Not surprisingly, the information leaked out to the newspapers several months ago."

"How did the authorities know it was Jason who killed Christopher?"

"Six months ago, he was arrested for killing his girlfriend. The murder was witnessed by a local reporter. That was when his real identity became known and the link to Christopher's murder was made. Unfortunately, Jason escaped custody while awaiting trial for his girlfriend's murder and later managed to kidnap Lily. Though the FBI team rescued Lily, Jason escaped with the ransom money, killing an agent in the process."

The piece of roll in Linda's fingers crumbled. "Was Emmett part of that FBI team?"

"Yes. He wants to stop his brother as much—more, I'm sure—than anyone."

"But—but—" One agent on the team had already been killed. Jason Jamison had already murdered one of his brothers. What if Emmett was hurt? What if Emmett…?

That dangerous flood of emotions filled her again. Concern, fear, a sharp pang of grief that had no place for a man who was still alive. For a man she barely knew.

But what if something happened to Emmett?

Linda tried pushing back the welling feelings, but they weren't under her control. Her body trembled and she felt that sting of tears once again in her eyes.

"Nan, I…" Linda swallowed, trying to strengthen her voice so that she could get out some excuse. Any excuse that would take her out of the house and away from the other woman before she guessed that Linda's recovery was shaky at best. She had to get well, be well, because she owed so much to everyone and she had so much to take charge of, including—

"Ricky!" Nan exclaimed, a smile in her voice. "Ricky's home. Look, there he is, out in the garden."

"Ricky?" Had so much time passed? Linda blinked away the incipient tears to check her watch. "It's only one o'clock."

"Minimum day," Nan replied. Her fond gaze was directed out the window. "He's growing like a weed, don't you think?"

Linda stared through the glass at the boy. Her son. He was looking taller than before, she supposed. His arms and fingers long, too. "I saw him on traffic patrol duty Friday," she said.

He was fooling around with that ubiquitous Hacky Sack he always seemed to carry. His blond hair rippled as he bounced the little ball up and down on the inner surface of his foot. Two butterflies flew into the picture he made, their yellow wings as bright as the little boy's hair. Their fluttering movements were almost as uneven as the new beat of her pounding heart.

He was beautiful, that little boy.

Her son.

The thought was almost too much. The flood that she'd been holding out against threatened to break down the gates she'd erected. She squeezed shut her eyes, took a deep breath, then opened them.

And now with the boy was the man. The golden boy was smiling up at the dark-haired man, at Emmett, who reached through those circling butterflies to ruffle the yellow silk of Ricky's hair. The gesture was friendly and tender and...perfect.

Perfectly suited to crash those gates and let in the flood that filled her with emotions that were hard to identify and harder even to breathe through. Concern, sympathy, uncertainty, fear.

Her son with half a parent.

Emmett with a damaged family.

"Linda, dear." Nan pressed a fresh napkin into Linda's hand. "You're crying."

She lifted her hand to her wet face, then looked away from the tableau outside the window to face Nan. She couldn't cover this up. "I'm sorry. It's the head injury again. They call it flooding. I wish I didn't feel so much but I...I can't help it."

Nan gave her a gentle smile. "Nobody's rushing you, Linda. No one expects you to be anything or anyone but who you are."

"But—"

"But you need to remember we care about you and always will. Though I'm afraid I don't buy this diagnosis of your tears."

Linda wiped at the last of them with the soft napkin. "It's the head injury."

"Like a Hallmark commercial is a head injury." Nan laughed. "Being touched emotionally by a tragic story or the sight of your son in the sunshine isn't about being injured, Linda. It's about being a woman."

It's about being a woman.

Linda glanced back out the window, just as Emmett looked inside. His green gaze caught hers, held it. She remembered again the feel of his lips on hers, his strong, wide hand on her shoulder.

And she worried that being a woman wasn't something she could ever recover from.

Chapter 5

A few days later, Linda awoke to strange, cooking-type sounds from the kitchen. Emmett wasn't a big-breakfast person, so she lay there, trying to think if there was something going on that day she had yet to remember. Nothing came to mind.

Lifting herself onto one elbow, she glanced at the open notebook on her bedside table.

Today is Sunday.

There was nothing beyond that simple phrase, which meant she had no specific plans for the day. Which meant she should make plans to spend time with Ricky. Just the thought made her feel anxious and inadequate, so she rolled back onto her pillow and considered going back to sleep. But the noises from the kitchen contin-ued, so curiosity prompted her to climb out of bed and slip into her robe. She was reaching for the doorknob when there was a light rap on the door itself.

Pulling it open, she faced no one, until she dropped her gaze from adult level to child level. There stood Ricky, a tray in his hands, an uncertain expression on his face. "Happy Mother's Day?" he said, more as a question than a greeting.

"I— Oh." Linda swallowed her surprise and shuffled back. *Mother's Day.* "Thank you."

Ricky's mouth moved into a small scowl. "It's supposed to be breakfast in bed," he said, jerking his chin toward the tray.

"Oh! Well, I…" This was a test, Linda realized in dismay. This was a test and she'd already failed the first question. "I'm sorry. I didn't know…."

"No harm done." It was Emmett, coming up behind the boy. "Scoot back under the covers and then Ricky can serve you as he'd planned."

Linda couldn't move fast enough. She followed the directions, sliding between the sheets, robe and all. Then she looked over at Ricky, trying to appear expectant instead of nervous. "This is such a pleasant surprise."

Ricky gave a little roll of his eyes, and her stomach dipped. She sounded stilted and formal, even to her own ears. Another red mark. She kept silent as he settled the tray onto her thighs.

"You have juice and coffee, and Emmett helped me make pancakes and bacon. He said you'd like them." The little boy's gaze challenged her for the truth.

"I *do* like them. Thank you, thank you very much." She lifted the napkin off the tray to reveal something made of construction paper and crayons. "What's this?"

Ricky backed away from the bed and stared down

at his shoes. "A dumb card they made us do in school. My teacher likes us to do dumb projects."

Linda picked it up. "It doesn't look dumb to me."

"It's dumb," Ricky said. "Really, really dumb."

She looked over the card. Apparently Ricky had inherited his artistic talent from her, which meant, unfortunately, no talent whatsoever. But what the stick figures and boxy structures on the face of the card lacked in verisimilitude, he'd made up for with a riotous use of color. The sky was very, very blue, the sun a blaze of orangeish yellow, and one of the persons depicted had a wealth of long, wheat-colored hair.

"Is this me?" she asked, hazarding a guess as she pointed.

"You *are* pretty skinny," Ricky said, glancing over at the collection of twiglike arms and legs that made up his rendition.

"But this breakfast is going to help with that," Linda said. Glancing up, she caught the glint of laughter in Emmett's eyes and had to bite the inside of her cheek to keep her own giggle back. The sad news was, the stick figure did bear a striking resemblance to her thin body.

She set the card on the bedside table beside her journal and sipped the juice and coffee, then took appreciative bites of the bacon and pancakes. Ricky watched her from the corner of his eyes, even as the toe of his left shoe was trying to dig a hole to China.

"This is all very good," she assured him. "I don't think I've ever had breakfast in bed before."

"Yeah?" He looked up, his expression pleased, then glanced away. "It was just some dumb idea that Nan had."

"I'll have to thank her," Linda said. Just another in

the long list of things she was grateful to the other woman for. "You had to get up early, too."

"It's better than the other years," he blurted out, then bent down to take up an extensive investigation of the broken shoelace on his sneaker.

Linda swallowed the bite of bacon. "Other years?"

"The other years I visited you on Mother's Day," he mumbled, head still bent over his shoe.

Linda's heart tightened, squeezing out tears that she struggled to hold inside. "You came to see me on other Mother's Days?"

"All of 'em, I guess," the boy said, straightening. "I made you lots of other cards, too. But you didn't know me…or you didn't care."

"Ricky." Emmett put a hand on the boy's shoulder. "You know—"

"It's all right," Linda said quickly. "I'm sure it felt that way to you, Ricky, that I didn't care about waking up and getting to know you. I wish I remembered all those other Mother's Day visits, too."

His face flushed, the color a bright pink against the golden gleam of his hair. "It was a dumb thing to say. I know you couldn't wake up."

"I couldn't. I don't know why not, or why I finally did wake up, but I'm certainly happy about it, even though it means getting to know you when you're practically all grown up."

He smiled at that, just a quick flash of white. "I'm not *all* grown up."

"Practically." Though it hurt to say it. It might be a slight exaggeration, but sometimes she thought he was at least too grown up for them to establish a true parent-child relationship. She was afraid that he was too grown up for her to ever feel as if he were truly her child. And that she was truly his mother.

"Practically all grown up," he repeated, as if he was trying out the sound of it. "Practically all grown up."

"And I have souvenirs of those other Mother's Days, even though I don't remember your actual visits."

Ricky frowned. "What kind of souvenirs?"

She opened the drawer of the bedside table and rummaged through the items placed inside. Nan was continually handing over things she thought Linda would like: photos, class work of Ricky's, art projects. Linda's first instinct had been to refuse them, because they reminded her of how much she'd lost and how much she might never gain, but she was glad now that she'd been too polite to ever say no.

"Here they are," she said, pulling out a stack of construction paper. "I have every Mother's Day card you ever made. I just didn't realize you'd delivered them to me in person."

The surprise got Ricky to take a step closer and then to take a seat on the edge of the bed. Linda looked over his head toward Emmett, who had retreated to lounge against the doorjamb, his hands thrust in his jeans pocket, his green eyes on her face. He gave her a little nod, and she felt some of her tension ease. This part of the test was going easier.

She and Ricky went through the cards together, chuckling at the kindergarten spelling in one and the liberal use of glitter on another. Ricky grumbled about the illustrations not improving much over the years. Apparently, his best friend Anthony could draw a Spider-Man and a Gambit well enough for comic books.

She leaned close to Ricky. "It's a Faraday failing,"

she murmured. "We're great with numbers, but we suck at art."

His eyes lit up. "You said *suck*," he crowed. "Nan and Dean don't allow me to say *suck*."

Linda let out a little bleat of distress. "*Suck* is bad? Oh, my gosh, of course *suck* is bad." Why was *suck* bad? It didn't matter; it only meant another ten points off her test score. "I must have seen it on TV. Don't tell Nan I said it, okay?"

Ricky was still giving her an unholy grin. "I won't rat on you. But can I say *suck* when I'm over here?"

"Of course not." She sent a pleading look toward Emmett, who was wearing a grin as unholy as Ricky's. "It was a slip of the tongue on my part, and neither one of us will say it ever again."

"Ah, you're no fun."

Linda frowned. "Well, I'm…" Sorry? Glad? Mothers of little boys weren't supposed to be fun, right? Fun mothers allowed *suck* and then they allowed no curfews and then they had to make monthly visits to their sons at the state penitentiary. But she *wanted* to be fun. For ten years, she'd been like a vegetable in Ricky's life. Now that she was awake, she didn't want to be the one who always insisted he eat them.

"Maybe we could do something fun today," she ventured.

"Like what?"

"Soccer?" That was easy. The kid was crazy about soccer. "You could teach me how to play. I was a pretty mean kickball player in my time."

Ricky was shaking his head. "It's not the same thing at all. You gotta use the side of your foot to kick the ball in soccer. And you can't touch it, ever. Unless you're the goalie, of course. The goalie gets to touch the ball with his hands."

"See, there's a lot you could help me with."

Ricky seemed to be considering the idea. "Okay. I'll help you learn soccer, if you help me with my book report."

Linda's pulse beat hard. This was what mothers did. Kicked the soccer ball around. Helped with book reports. But she knew that appearing too eager—and to be honest, she wasn't exactly sure how eager she actually was—would dock more points from her final score.

So she pretended to think it over. "I don't know. Does it require drawing? Because, as I just told you, the Faradays—"

"Suck at art." Ricky started laughing.

"Hey, wait a minute—"

"You said it. You said the Faradays suck at art."

"And I *said* we wouldn't use that word again." She looked over at Emmett who, instead of backing her up, was laughing, too.

"He has you there, Linda, you have to admit it."

"Mothers admit nothing," she said, trying to sound stern. "And if I hear that word again, there will be no soccer and no help on the book report."

Ricky sobered. "You have to help on the book report. It's *Old Yeller,* and Nan and Dean don't like books where the dog dies."

"Nobody likes books where the dog dies," Emmett put in.

"But everybody likes a good book report," Linda said. "So we'll restrain ourselves from using the wrong words and apply ourselves to writing a report on a book in which the dog dies."

Ricky turned to look at Emmett. "She's starting to

sound like a mother." It wasn't clear if that was a good thing or not.

"So she is."

"Then why don't I keep on my roll here and suggest you go back to the house, have your breakfast and give me time to shower and change. Then come back with paper, pencil and *Old Yeller*."

The boy scampered off.

Sighing, Linda looked over at Emmett. "The dog really dies?"

He nodded.

"I'm not going to like this."

"But you're going to do great at it. You *did* great."

"I'd give myself a C. Maybe."

"It's a start."

"You think? I'm not sure he's seeing me as a mother or more as a…big sister or something like that."

"It's a start, like I said. I think the relationship shows great potential."

But did she have what it took to finish the job? she thought as Emmett came farther into the room. Could she walk into this little boy's life and ever feel like his mother? *Be* his mother?

The mattress sagged as Emmett sat in the place where Ricky had been. The room suddenly felt smaller, hotter, more confining. Across the remains on the breakfast tray and the scattered, homemade cards, she met Emmett's gaze.

And that feeling of being tested came over her again.

Awareness thickened the air in the room. She'd never before seen the heat in the color green, but she saw it now, knew it now in the depths of Emmett's eyes.

He hadn't touched her in days, not since that one kiss in the kitchen, but it was as if the intervening time evaporated. It seemed like only seconds ago, the blink of an eye ago, that his lips had been on hers.

"Linda," he started, staring at her mouth. "Should we...?"

Should we...kiss again? Or avoid it altogether? A test, she reminded herself. This was another test. And though she'd done average work with Ricky that morning, she wasn't prepared to face another rigorous examination.

She broke their gazes and the bonds of the unwelcome, uncomfortable attraction by leaping out of bed. "I better get ready for Ricky," she declared, rushing toward the bathroom.

"Coward," she thought she heard him say.

But it could just as easily have been herself speaking.

Emmett left the house while Ricky and Linda worked on the *Old Yeller* book report. He'd already experienced too much death in his life and even without that, he hated stories in which a dog died as much as the next man. It was late afternoon when he reentered the guest house. The distant tapping told him that Linda was working on the computer set up on a desk in one corner of the living room. He walked in just as one of her palms slammed flat on the keyboard.

The image on the screen fractured into pieces that spun out into the lonely regions of a black galaxy. She bowed her neck until her forehead was resting on her forearm in a posture telegraphing exhaustion, frustration or despair. Maybe all of the above.

She let out a long sigh.

At the sound, compassion stabbed him. Emmett took an instinctive step back.

Back off. Get out. Get away.

He'd had enough of pain in the past few months. While he'd promised Ryan he'd help her, he didn't need to be drawn into her emotional world. Every time he let himself be vulnerable to that, he ended up being vulnerable to *her.*

Help her. That was what he was here for. Wanting to hold her, comfort her, kiss her was a damn stupid, nonsensical compulsion.

Yes, there was an undeniable physical attraction between the two of them, but she didn't appear to be eager to explore it. And he didn't want to think that he was exploiting it. A woman who'd been "asleep" for ten years had to be out of practice in the ways of men and women. She wasn't ready for a flirtation, let alone a fling, which was all he had to offer.

He took another step back and bumped into a side table, its legs clattering against the hardwood floor. Linda jumped at the sound, spinning in her chair to confront him. "Emmett!" She held her hand to her throat. "You scared me."

You scare me, too, honey, he thought. That beautiful blond hair, those blue eyes and those delicate features seemed to have been put together with the express purpose of dissolving his good intentions.

He wanted to hold her, comfort her, kiss her.

But he wasn't going to do it. So he cleared his throat and cocked an eyebrow at the computer screen. "Book report making you crazy?"

She glanced at the screen, still showing that black void with only a few pinprick stars to alleviate its darkness. "No, that went okay. I was playing one of the dexterity games they sent home with me from rehab."

He'd seen her practice them before. Some appeared to be logic-type word problems, while the ones that caused her shoulders to tense and her jaw to harden were the manual dexterity games that seemed like snazzier versions of the original Pac-Man and Asteroids. "The Evil Blaster obliterate all your rocket ships?"

"I don't want to talk about it. It makes me want to hit something. What about you? Did you have a pleasant afternoon?"

"I took a drive out to Ryan's ranch in Red Rock." He couldn't believe he'd told her.

"To visit Lily?"

He shook his head. "Just to…to look at the land."

"To visit Ryan."

He stared at her. How did she know? "But Ryan isn't there," he said, his voice suddenly harsh. Ryan was nowhere, just as his brother Christopher was nowhere, just as Jessica Chandler was nowhere. His wanting it to be otherwise didn't change a damn thing.

Love didn't wake the dead. Jessica's father had told him that when Emmett had gone to the Chandler home to tell him she'd been found. *She* hadn't been found, John Chandler had corrected him. She was lost forever, no matter how much they cared for her, no matter how much and for how long they would grieve. Love didn't wake the dead.

"Your memories of Ryan are there, at the ranch."

It was Linda talking again, and he transferred his focus to her face. "I don't want to talk about it."

"Because it makes you want to hit something? I can relate to that." The rueful tone in her voice prodded him again, sending another shot of sympathy pain through him. "The injury makes me feel so horribly defenseless sometimes, as if there were some dark force waiting out there, around the corner or on the other side of the window, to yank me back into the murky twilight."

Since he was already there in that murky twilight, had been there since he'd heard of Christopher's death, he knew exactly what she meant. While his father had bodily hauled him out of the dingy cabin in the Sandia Mountains, his spirit still dwelled in the darkness.

He didn't wish that life in the shadows on anyone. He didn't want her to even fear it.

"Maybe we can do something about that vulnerability," he said, remembering her telling him she used to be tough and that she wanted to be tough again. "We can do something about your urge to hit something at the same time, too. You know anything about martial arts?"

"Martial arts?"

"You know, Jackie Chan? Or think *Crouching Tiger, Hidden Dragon.*"

She blinked her beautiful blue eyes at him. "Jackie Chan? Crouching dragons? I don't know what you're talking about."

Of course she wouldn't. She'd been in that twilight world when the martial arts hero Jackie Chan had come to fame and the movie *Crouching Tiger, Hidden Dragon* had hit the theaters. "Tonight we have some DVDs to rent. But in the meantime, how about a little hand-to-hand sparring, secret agent accountant?"

The nickname had her smiling, which in turn made him almost smile, as well. "Okay," she said. "I guess I'm game."

A few minutes later, they met in the workout room on the mat he'd laid out, both of them in sweatpants and T-shirts. Linda didn't look as if she'd any second thoughts. Her eyes were bright as she captured her hair into a ponytail.

"What are you going to teach me?" she asked. "I

don't remember all the different styles, but there's a lot of them, right? Jujitsu, karate, tae kwon do…"

"Despite their historical roots, today many of the disciplines are mainly taught for competition and display," he replied. "I'm going to teach you how to street fight."

Her eyes went wide, but she didn't say anything more. Instead, he found himself filling the silence with all the admonitions he wished he could have given to every victim he'd encountered or been too late to help in the last half-dozen years. He talked quickly, as if he had to get it all out before an expiration date.

"When it comes to being on the streets, don't walk like a victim. Whenever he can, a criminal avoids those who appear determined and purposeful. They look for the unaware and helpless. Nervous about someone you see? Look them in the eye. Let them know you are aware of them and if you had to, you could identify them later. Never turn your back on someone who feels like a threat."

Linda was running the palms of her hands up and down the fabric covering her thighs. It was a slightly anxious gesture, but he thought of her feeling vulnerable and he thought of all the defenseless people he'd met in his lifetime and continued with his lecture. "All repair or delivery or inspection persons should set up an appointment with you by phone, in advance, and carry photo ID. Check it thoroughly before you open your door to them. If someone gets into your house, know that any weapons in your home might be used against you. Finally, most importantly, heed your instincts. Those warning bells going off in your head are *not* paranoia. Your senses are more powerful than you know and you should listen to them. But…"

She swallowed. "But?"

"But if you get caught in a bad situation, you can be smart enough and tough enough to help yourself get out of it."

"And one session with you will improve my odds?"

"Probably not. And probably the paranoid one is me, but I'd like to see you, I'd like to see everyone, take a rigorous self-defense course that stresses awareness first, running like hell second, and any kind of combat as a last resort."

Linda nodded slowly. "I think I'd like to do that. But for now, what can you teach me?"

He nodded back. "If you like, we can do a little every day."

The attacks he prepared her for had to be the obvious ones—the shove, the headlock, the hair pull—and the countermoves easy to execute and remember. Nothing fancy. He focused on simplicity as he showed them to her, reminding her time and again that in a real situation she would likely be facing someone larger than herself and certainly more aggressive. She was breathing hard after thirty minutes, even though the simple defenses he demonstrated were based not on strength, but smarts.

"And then there's the pinch," he told her as they faced each other across the mat. "Never underestimate the pinch." He explained that pressing a thin fold of an attacker's skin between her forefinger and the harder surface of the second knuckle of the thumb could surprise and pain an assailant enough to give her the needed moments to get free and away. "Some of the best targets are the inside and back of the upper arms, the sides of the upper chest near the armpits, the inside of either leg from just above the knee all the way to the groin, the fold of skin between the upper lip and nose, and the male genitals."

She grimaced. Her hair was slipping from the rubber band, and she reached up to secure it more tightly. "I don't think I want to practice pinching you... anywhere."

But he thought it was time for her to practice something else. Without giving her a word of warning, he lunged at her for a football tackle, his arms reaching out to grab her around the thighs.

She made a little blurp of surprise, then grabbed his waist with both hands. If he had been wearing a belt it would have been easier for her, but still she followed what they'd practiced and shifted her feet and body back, loosening his grip on her thighs. Now leverage favored her, and she bore down across the top of his back, forcing his body down and slamming his face into the mat.

He lay there, arms out to his sides, Linda draped over him, her head in the small of his back.

"Move up," he ordered her, his voice thick. "Move up and away."

She leapt to her feet. "Oh, my God. I've hurt you! Are you all right? Should I call a doctor?"

"No, I'm fine." Clearing his throat, he sat up. "Once you've got the attacker down, you need to get as far away from him as possible. Slam his face to the floor, then run, okay?"

She hunkered down to study him. "Are you sure you're all right?" Her hands patted at his shoulders and chest. "I didn't hurt something?"

"Not even my ego. I want you to get good at this, remember?" Okay, so his ears were ringing a little and his ego might be slightly dented, but she didn't need to know that. "You did great, Linda."

She dropped to the mat beside him and gave him a grin that was brighter than summer sunshine. "I did, didn't I? I bested you." Her hand came up and gave him a little playful shove to the shoulder. He let it take him over, flat onto his back.

He managed to take her with him. "You're not the only one with smooth moves," he said, looking into her surprised eyes. She was half lying on his chest, her blond hair a curtain around her face. She was flushed and her eyes were still sparkling; he knew that he'd improved her mood and upped her level of confidence.

He'd helped her. There was no longer a reason to want to hold her, comfort her, kiss her.

But she was in his arms, and the comfort he was feeling seemed to be his, and the urge to kiss her was stronger than before. Once again, it was her fortitude that fascinated him. Instead of curling into a fetal position when life wasn't easy, she'd actually straightened out of such a position to reclaim her life.

She *was* tough.

"What did you say about those warning bells going off in my head?" she murmured, her gaze trained on his face. "That they're *not* paranoia?"

He had to smile at that. "You think I'm dangerous to you?"

"Not in the way that you mean."

Emmett refused to let his fingers tighten on her shoulders. Instead, he kept his grasp light, feeling the damp warmth of her skin through the T-shirt. "I won't hurt you, Linda."

She nodded. "You certainly won't mean to."

"Then I should let you go." Despite the knowledge

that he should do just that, neither one of them moved a muscle.

"I've been an orphan since I first left for college at sixteen." It was a statement of fact.

"That must have been rough." He thought her confidence required that he share one of his own. "I've been pretty much estranged from my own family since I left home. The events of the past nine months have put us in contact again, but we're not any closer than before."

"I think I was pretty lonely, which was why I joined the Treasury Department after college."

"I thought that was because you wanted to be a secret agent accountant."

She made a face. "I should have known I'd live to regret telling you that. More than being a secret agent, I was looking to be part of a team...a family of sorts."

"Interesting. I did my best to run away from my family." The animosity between his two older brothers and the tension it had brought into his parents' home had been something he'd wanted to escape from for as long as he could remember.

"But going undercover at Fortune TX, Ltd. left me on my own."

"And prey to Cameron." Emmett instantly regretted the words.

Linda only looked thoughtful. "Maybe. I don't know. I don't think I'll ever know, since I can't remember much about that time and since I'm not that same twenty-two-year-old, no matter that the years passed without my really living them."

They were still chest to chest and, oddly, it felt like the right way to be when trading confessions. Except... "Why are you telling me this?"

"I don't think I'm any good with men."

He blinked. "Inexperience isn't quite the same as not being any good."

She shrugged. "I don't have enough experience to know."

"What are you getting at, Linda?"

Her breath came in, then released in a long exhale. It pushed her soft breasts against his chest. His body hardened and he was grateful for the stretchy fabric of his sweats. This would have been hell in a tight pair of jeans.

"I'm saying, Emmett, that I *think* I know why we're lying here on the floor together, but I'm not sure exactly what to do about it and whether where it's leading would be very satisfying for either one of us."

Did she mean leading to sex? Or to a relationship? One he was pretty damn confident he could handle; the other was completely out of the question.

So he put her away from him and sat up. "Okay, then, it's like I said. Combat as a last resort." He stood.

"Yes," she murmured as he left the room. "It *is* like you said. Awareness first, running like hell second."

Chapter 6

Emmett figured that if Linda could drive herself—something she was working toward—she wouldn't have allowed him to chauffeur her to Ricky's soccer game a few days later. Earlier, on their way to another appointment, Nan and Dean had dropped the boy off for a quick pregame practice, so there was no one to interrupt the steady, heavy silence between Emmett and Linda.

Though they'd continued to coexist in the guest house without argument and had even practiced on the mat once again, the tension between them was rising with each hour.

He still didn't know if she thought he'd rejected her when they'd been breast to chest that afternoon on the mat. But even if she did, he wasn't going to correct her impression. Anything that kept them apart and kept them from unleashing this latent sexual energy on each other was something to be nurtured, not destroyed.

He glanced over at her. "I'll drop you off and then I'm going to pick up someone else. I think she'll like to see the game."

Linda kept her gaze trained out the window. "She? You're bringing a date?" Her voice was chilly, and very, very polite. "That's nice, but please don't think you have to spend your time with a woman babysitting me. Ricky and I can find someone to bring us back to the house."

He rolled his eyes. "It's not—" Deciding against explaining, he closed his mouth. In a few moments, they'd reached the field and she exited the car without a smile, a second glance, without anything beyond a thank-you. It left him free, however, to watch her walk away from him without her knowledge.

She looked damn good, mouthwateringly good, in a pair of butt-hugging shorts, her long legs naked of everything but a pair of flimsy sandals. Her flag of blond hair fluttered in the breeze and he might have stared all day if a car hadn't come up behind him and honked.

It only took him a short time to collect his "date" and return with her to the soccer field. With Nan and Dean unable to attend the game, he'd thought of bringing the other woman. Not only would she provide a much-needed buffer between himself and Linda, he'd figured she would welcome the outing.

"Lily!" Linda exclaimed, as she saw the other woman climbing up into the stands. The glance she cast at Emmett stopped just short of a glare. "No one told me you were coming to the game." She stood up and gave Lily a hug. "How are you?" she said softly. "I am so happy you're here. Ricky will be, too."

Lily Fortune, a widow of just a few short weeks, was close to sixty, Emmett knew. Grief and the rigors of her recent kidnapping at Jason's hands had added more heavy threads of silver to her dark hair, but she remained a fine-looking woman. As she sat down on the wooden bench, she pulled on a pair of dark sunglasses to cover her large, tilted brown eyes and then linked her arm with Linda's. "I'm getting by," she said, "by keeping myself busy with activities like lunches with old friends—why I was in San Antonio today— and the important soccer matches of my favorite ten-year-old boy."

Emmett seated himself on Lily's other side. "And you're busy with the arrangements for the upcoming Fortune reunion, right? I heard that you're going through with that."

Linda's eyes rounded. "Lily, no. You can't want to take on such a big project right now."

"It's exactly a big project that I need," the older woman said, her voice firm. "It keeps me busy and I like the idea of everyone finally getting together."

"There were Fortunes galore—" Emmett stopped himself.

"At Ryan's memorial service," Lily finished matter-of-factly. "But this is different. This is going to be a happy occasion."

Emmett scoffed to himself. Happy occasion? Unless they rounded up Jason in the next couple of weeks, there were going to be plenty of dark thoughts at that happy occasion. "I'll get him," he muttered to himself.

But Lily heard him. "Of course you will. But I won't let even Jason ruin the big party I have planned. Well, that Ryan planned, really. It was his dream."

Emmett couldn't disagree with that. Years before, in the 1970s, Ryan had been reunited with the family of Patrick Fortune, his cousin in New York. Patrick and his wife, Lacey, had five children, all whom had spent summers in Texas and who had ultimately settled near Ryan.

The previous November, after Jason had been jailed for the murder of his girlfriend Melissa and then implicated in Christopher's death, Ryan had been contacted by Emmett's father, Blake. It was Blake who had explained why the hereditary, distinctive Fortune birthmark had been found on Christopher's body—Blake's father and Ryan's father had been half brothers. Ryan had immediately embraced what was left of the Jamison clan, despite the trouble Jason Jamison had brought to the area. And even after Jason had kidnapped his beloved Lily.

Ryan had been a man whose appreciation for family ran very, very deep.

"Emmett?" Lily put a cool hand on his arm. "Are you all right?"

He blinked away the bright sunshine's sting, then avoided meeting her gaze by seeking Ricky on the field. The game was just about to start and it wasn't hard to find the boy's sunny hair. "Looks like he's playing goalie this quarter," he said, watching him pull on a shirt different from the others on his team.

"Goalie?" Linda's voice sounded panicked. *"Goalie?"*

Emmett tried placating her. "You've seen him play before. He's a great goalie. He won't be hurt."

"It's not about him getting physically hurt." Linda bounced up from her seat. "I can't sit when he plays goalie. Do you realize what happens when a boy plays goalie? If the ball goes in, he gets all the blame!"

"No—"

"Yes, I've seen it happen. And then they look over at the boy's mother and the boy's mother feels as if she needs to do two things—grab her kid up into her arms and then disappear into a hole in the earth." She started clattering down the bench seats. "I need to take a little walk."

Emmett half rose to follow her, but Lily put her hand on his arm again. "Let her go. This sports-watching can take practice—and lots of little walks."

"That's right," he said, settling back onto the bench. "I'm sure you've done your share of this kind of thing."

"Baseball and ballet. Soccer games and school plays. My girls, Hannah and Maria, were involved in everything. My son, Cole, was a sports fanatic. Honing his competitive skills for his grown-up life as a lawyer, I suppose."

Emmett had met the older man at the memorial service a few weeks ago and knew something else about him, as well. "Ryan told me Cole is Ricky's half brother. Cameron was his father, too."

Lily nodded. "That's the truth, and an old, old story. But Ricky has some other half siblings as well, Cameron's children with his wife, Mary Ellen. You've met Holden and Logan, of course, who both work at Fortune TX, Ltd. Their sister, Eden, is married to Sheikh Ben Ramir. With Linda's permission, of course, I'd like to introduce Ricky to all of them at the reunion—as their little brother."

Emmett looked at the older woman. "Is that such a good idea? We've kept it a secret until now. That was Ryan's decision."

"A decision he made ten years ago, when he didn't want it to get out what Cameron had done. But the years have passed, and his other children have matured and come to grips with the man their father was. I have told someone else about Ricky's parentage—my niece,

Susan Fortune, who is a psychologist and experienced with children. She agrees with me that Ricky could benefit from the truth. Don't you think he would feel more secure with the knowledge he had a real place in this family, beyond friendship? And real brothers and a sister who will look out for him all his life?"

Emmett sighed. "I'm not the one you should ask about sibling relationships, obviously."

"Oh, dear." Lily frowned at him. "I didn't want to bring up painful memories for you."

But they were always there, lying just below the surface, ready to grab him like monsters he'd imagined under his bed as a kid. "I'm just not in the mood to think about parties right now, Lily. I'm sorry."

She was prevented from answering by the hail of an older couple seated farther down in the stands. They came over to Lily to exchange hugs and express their condolences and how much they missed Ryan. From there, a parade of well-wishers found their way to her all with glowing praise for her husband and sympathy for his widow.

Emmett had to distance himself from the emotions swirling around him. Though he remained in place, he focused on the game, silently rooting for Ricky's team. The kid was a great player, talented all around, and Emmett found himself gripping his own knee as a ball rolled dangerously close to the goal box. But Ricky scrambled for it and kicked it far down the field.

Smiling at the boy's success, Emmett searched the area for Linda. He spied her at the far end of the grass, leaning against the cyclone fencing, her fingers hooked into the wire diamond patterns. She was smiling, too, and he caught her eye and gave her a thumbs-up sign. She flashed him one back, but low at her side, in case, he thought, Ricky was watching. She already knew a mother shouldn't be too effusive.

He laughed out loud.

"That's something I've been waiting to hear," Lily said, her mouth curving up.

"What?"

"You, Emmett Jamison, laughing."

He rubbed his hand over his hair. "I'm not much of a ha-ha sort of guy. It's not been much of a ha-ha time in my life." Already he felt guilty for even that small release.

"You're not to blame for anything, Emmett. You're much too sensible for that."

"How about for my brother getting away from us? I should have been able to stop him."

Lily was shaking her head. "But Ryan would still be gone now, wouldn't he? He wouldn't want you wasting your time on what-could-have-beens."

"Maybe I've been wasting my time with Linda and Ricky," he muttered. "I've let them derail me from my pursuit of Jason."

"Oh, is that right?" Lily scoffed. "I have my contacts, too, young man, and I happen to know you're in daily communication with the FBI team and the police working this case. They told me about Jason's taunting call to you and that they've encouraged you to lie low and wait for him to make another. All the other leads are exhausted."

"*I* haven't exhausted them. Maybe if I—"

"You know you're doing the right thing. Even your cousin Collin agrees."

Emmett made an impatient gesture. "Collin's derailed himself, thanks to Lucy. A woman can do that to a man."

"Is that what Linda has done to you, Emmett?"

"Linda…" Linda seemed to be his punishment these days. She was so beautiful, so sexy; she had so much that he could admire—her courage, her ability to build a new life for herself and her son. His attraction to her only hurt, because he knew it wasn't right to pursue her. "Linda needs protection."

"From you? I doubt that."

"She hasn't been around a man in years. I wouldn't want to give her the wrong idea."

"Why, Emmett." Lily was smiling at him now. "I wouldn't have guessed you to be so sexist. Don't you think she's smart enough to make up her own mind about you and what she wants from you?"

"I didn't say she isn't smart!" He knew she was smart. And funny. *Secret agent accountant.* And so damn sexy. His gaze was drawn to her again, and he watched the way the breeze plastered her thin T-shirt to her breasts. She'd gained weight, too, he thought, and in a good way. "I don't want her to think that I'm planning on staying around."

Lily's smile turned sly. "Maybe, just maybe, that isn't the kind of staying power she's interested in."

He looked over, eyebrows raised. "I'm not sure how I should take that, Lily."

"With the best of intentions, Emmett. I want you—Ryan and I both want you—to be happy. To reach out to life, really live the moment, instead of wallowing in all the ugliness."

He frowned. "You make me sound like a pig in mud."

"Nope. Pigs are happy creatures. Come out to the ranch and I'll show you."

"I'm—" Happy, he wanted to say, but he couldn't.

Happiness always seemed to be out of his reach, a daydream, a fantasy, nothing substantial enough to stay.

"What are you two talking about?"

Linda was back, smelling like a fresh breeze and with a smile on her face. "Ricky's sitting out the next quarter, so I can relax for a while."

"We're talking about Emmett," Lily said. "And how he should reach out for what he wants."

Linda stilled. Her gaze leapt to Emmett's and there was that hum between them, a sexual connection that was like a long fuse, burning at both ends, with a bomb in the middle. He couldn't imagine the potential explosion. But God, he wanted to let it rock his world.

"I think he should reach out, too," Linda said, her gaze not leaving his. "Reach out and discover exactly what's there, right at the end of his fingertips."

Yeah, he could imagine the explosion, Emmett amended. And he was so tempted to let it rock his world.

Maybe because she'd survived her mother-of-soccer-goalie quarter, maybe because Lily had seemed so serene, maybe because of the warm, late afternoon air, as the soccer game ended, Linda found herself with full-on spring fever. With a smile on her face, she followed the older woman out of the stands and onto the field to form the traditional victory tunnel with the other parents. Lily faced another grandmotherly type to link hands above their heads, leaving Linda to face Emmett.

"Reach out and discover exactly what's there?" he murmured to her, holding up his arms.

She hesitated, feeling a flush crawl over her face. It was what she'd said to him in the stands during the game, and even with Lily as a chaperone, it had sounded to her own ears like a pretty straightforward invitation. *Reach out and touch* me.

That day on the mat, she'd offered herself to him, too. Okay, so she'd expressed a few doubts about it, as well, but she'd expected—no, wanted—him to ignore those and then show her exactly what their mutual desire could do to them both. But Emmett had been too much of the gentleman—no, protector—to take the lead when she'd shown uncertainty.

Which meant she was going to have to be a grownup and reach out herself if that was what she desired.

Slowly, she lifted her hands to meet his. At the contact, a rubber-band snap of awareness pinged through her system. He twined their fingers, and the hard maleness of his hands separating hers made her spine shiver and her stomach shimmy. His eyes were a darker green than the grass, and she remembered again how the emerald color could hold the yellow heat of a flame.

Ricky's team was still shaking hands with the opposing players. She glanced over at them, then back to Emmett. She licked her suddenly dry lips.

His fingers tightened on hers.

"Uh, great game, right?" she said.

"Once we made it through all the heavy breathing."

She frowned. "Heavy breathing?"

"You're pretty competitive, do you know that? I thought you were going to rush the ref at that offside call."

The heavy-breathing comment had distracted her. "Huh? What?" She flushed again, realizing she was now staring at his wide chest, trying to determine if his breathing was in any way affected by their shared touch. Enough air wasn't getting to *her* lungs. "I don't even know what offside means," she confessed. "I was just being loyal to the team."

"Offsides is all about positioning. And who gets to be ahead of whom on the way to the goal."

Was there a double entendre to that? She studied his face, trying to figure it out. What was the goal? Who was ahead? His noncommittal expression didn't provide any clues. But something about his chiseled features and those dark whiskers just starting to shadow his jaw made her go all shivery again.

She drew in a breath of the warm air and experienced another giddy rush of well-being that made her feel as if she could soar like the birds flying through the brilliant sky. Maybe her spring fever was sparking a hormone surge. That was only natural, right? And it would explain her overwhelming attraction to this man. Think about it—ten years of dormant sexuality coming alive all at once!

His hands squeezed hers. "Linda?"

She was going to have to tell him. She was going to have to ask for what she wanted from him…and hopefully get it. "Emmett—"

But the moment and her words were lost as Ricky's soccer team ran screaming through the tunnel of arms and bodies.

The moment was lost…but not her desire for Emmett.

It simmered away as he drove them back to the guest house, first dropping Lily off at a friend's, and then stopping to pick up Ricky's favorite ham-and-pineapple pizza. It wasn't yet dark when the three of them were gathered around the small kitchen table. There were streaks of dirt on Ricky's cheeks and the tips of his hair were stuck together with sweat.

"Maybe we should have you shower before eating," she said.

"My hands are clean, I washed them. See?" Ricky held them out. They did look clean, until you looked two inches beyond his wrists.

"Your elbows are grimy and you have dirt on your neck."

He rolled his eyes. "I don't eat pizza with my elbows or my neck, do I?"

"Ricky."

Just his name in Emmett's low, calm voice sent Ricky's shoulders into a slump. "Sorry," he said. "Is that what you want me to do? Shower?"

With his stomach rumbling and his favorite pizza fresh, she found she couldn't toe that maternal line. "No." Wouldn't a real mother sacrifice hot pizza for cleanliness? Her happy mood deflated. "I suppose you don't eat pizza with your elbows or your neck, do you?"

"Nope." He dug into the box and pulled out a cheesy slice. "I'll shower after dinner. Then you can quiz me on my spelling words."

Spelling she should be able to do, but her mood stayed glum. "Sure."

Emmett leaned close to pour some iced tea into Linda's glass. "Good call," he said, the words just a whisper against her ear.

Her temperature jacked high. Goose bumps skittered low. She darted a glance his way, but couldn't figure out if he knew his hot breath affected her or if he even cared.

What if the spring fever and hormone surge were all one-sided? What if the reason he'd left her on the mat that day wasn't because he was a gentleman but because he was too much a gentleman to out-and-out reject her?

If her brain had been scrambled for so long, didn't it stand to reason that her signals were crossed, as well?

She wasn't any better at men than she was at mothering, she thought morosely, and bit into her pizza.

Then Emmett touched her cheek with one fingertip. "Why so ferocious?"

Her head turned toward him, and his thumb went to the corner of her mouth. "You're oozing pizza sauce."

Oozing. Apt word, she thought, and watched him lick the dab of tomato from his thumb. Scrambled brains or not, desire was oozing out of her pores, radiating from her like heat from the summer sidewalk. "I want—" She stopped herself just short, remembering it was dinner, and still light out, and most of all, that her son shared the table with them.

One of Emmett's dark eyebrows flew up. "You want what?"

It took all she had to look away. "I'll…let you know," she said, applying herself to her pizza slice. She would. She had to, or else go crazy wondering what he wanted, what could be, what it would be like between them, if he was suffering the same symptoms she was.

After pizza, quizzing Ricky for the spelling test served as only more nerve-racking postponement. Though Linda was hyperaware of Emmett reading the newspaper at the kitchen table just a knee away, she cleared her throat and looked over the words. Ricky had his pencil poised over paper.

"How do I do this?"

The boy gave her one of his patented don't-you-know-anything looks but answered pleasantly enough. "Say the word. Use it in a sentence, then say the word again."

"Oh. Okay." Ten years in a coma, plus another ten

since she'd taken a spelling test, and apparently there had not been an evolution in spelling education. "That's just how it was for me."

"I'm good at spelling," Ricky said.

She smiled at him. "I was, too."

With tacit agreement, they both looked at Emmett. His gaze lifted, flickered from one face to the other, then back. "I take the fifth."

Ricky grinned. "You can take it, but I betcha can't spell it."

Linda had to laugh, even as Emmett sent her a pained look. "Control your kid," he said. "I take that back, control *yourself* and your kid."

Oh, but she wasn't going to do either. Ricky was laughing, she was laughing, there was a light in Emmett's eyes that she'd never seen before and she suspected it was suppressed laughter. They all needed that.

"Okay," she finally said, lifting her palm to glance at the list on the table. "First word. *Queen.* I am the queen bee. *Queen.*"

Ricky groaned, but bent his head over his page. "Next one."

"*Quilt.*" For a second, the word looked odd to her. *Quilt?* Then an image popped into her mind. "There is a pretty quilt on my bed. *Quilt.*"

Emmett rustled the newspaper. Maybe it was the sound, or maybe the mention of bed, but he drew her gaze again. She looked up from the spelling list and found that he was looking at her. Their gazes held.

"What's the next one?" Ricky prodded. "I don't want this to take all night."

"Me, either," Emmett said softly. "You need to get back to the house and we need to—"

Linda dropped her gaze, her heart beating wildly. *"Relax,"* she read aloud. "It's hard to relax when…"

"The room is so warm." Emmett finished for her.

"That doesn't make any sense," Ricky complained.

It did to Linda. She licked her lips and tried to focus on the words on the page but they were jumping like her pulse. She closed her eyes, opened them. *"Liquid,"* she said. "I feel liquid when—"

"Nobody *feels* liquid," Ricky corrected.

"Right, right. Sorry. Ice turns into a liquid when it, uh…uh…"

"Melts," Emmett supplied.

Oooh. She was melting, and her concentration was shot. Looking down at the spelling list, none of the jumble of letters was making any sense to her. The only thing that made sense was that expectant pounding of her heart. That fizz of anticipation in her blood.

She shoved the list toward Emmett. "I need a drink of water."

"Excellent," she heard him say as she strode toward the sink. "The man thought he had an excellent chance with the woman. *Excellent.*"

Ricky was making choking sounds. "No love sentences! Yuck!"

Her eyes closed and holding the cool glass against her cheek, Linda lingered near the sink as the two went through the words. *Quart. Change. Pledge.*

"Quick. The kid needed to get to sleep quick. *Quick.*"

"Why?" Ricky asked, writing down the word. "Maybe I should stay up late tonight."

"No. No way does the boy get to stay up late. No."

"That's not on the list," Ricky said, grinning.

"But the answer's true all the same." Emmett glanced over at Linda and she clutched her glass so she wouldn't shiver. "Only two more words and then it's bedtime at the big house for you."

"Go ahead," Ricky grumbled.

"*Excited.* He could tell that she was excited. *Excited.*"

"About what?" the little boy asked as he wrote down the word. "What's she excited about?"

Emmett glanced down at the list, then glanced over at Linda, a very male, almost smug half smile curving the corners of his usually hard mouth. "The upcoming *explosion,*" he answered. *"Explosion."*

At that, she almost ended up a liquid, melted puddle on the floor. But she held it together enough to wish Ricky good-night. Then, as Emmett escorted him back to Nan and Dean's, she ran for the bathroom. The bright light bouncing off the white walls hurt her eyes, but she squinted at the glare and managed to fumble her way through brushing her teeth. Twice.

She didn't have her signals crossed this time. Emmett wanted her just as much as she wanted him. For the first time in more than ten years, she was going to know what it was like to be in a man's arms.

The overhead light seemed to pulse as she stared at her reflection in the mirror. *Don't mess this up, Linda,* she told herself. *Don't mess this up.*

Chapter 7

Emmett lectured himself all the way to the big house and back. His conversation with Lily at the soccer game had let a little light into his soul and the look in Linda's eyes at the kitchen table had shed a little light onto what she was looking for with him. Lily had assured him that Linda wasn't necessarily interested in his ability to stick around, and that crackle in the atmosphere between them tonight seemed to prove what she *was* interested in.

But, Jamison, he reminded himself, *you will keep a lid on things. You will move slow and you will let this go as far as Linda wants it and no further. You will be sure that as physical as it might between us, that you won't let it be* intimate.

When he entered the guest house, he heard her in the bathroom and leaned his shoulders against the wall outside to wait for her. She pulled open the door, turning off the light at the same time, and gave a little start of surprise at finding him there.

"You," she said.

"You were expecting someone else?"

She slowly shook her head, even as a flush brushed across her beautiful cheekbones. "I only want you." Her face flushed darker.

He wouldn't let her be embarrassed by the admission. "That sounds good to me." Pushing away from the wall, he stepped toward her.

She looked as if she might flee, but then she smiled at him and took her own step. They were toe-to-toe. "Don't forget that I told you I was out of practice," she warned.

He didn't twitch a muscle, but he was aware of the heat of his body reaching toward hers and the mingling of their warm breaths. "It's like riding a bicycle."

Her pretty mouth pursed. "I haven't done that in more than ten years, either."

"Then that's for another day." His hands caught hers and he lightly twined their fingers, then brushed his thumbs across her knuckles. "Tonight is for us."

She shivered.

"Cold?" he whispered.

Her laugh sounded shaky, as her fingers clenched his. "Easy, I think. Your touch affects me in a pretty powerful way, Mr. Jamison."

He smiled. "In case you've forgotten, Ms. Faraday, that's exactly the way it's supposed to work." With a little tug, he pulled her nearer so that their hips were close and their lips even closer.

She looked up at him and winced.

"What is it?"

"The hall light. It's so bright."

"No problem." He reached out and flicked the switch. It wasn't completely dark now; illumination from the kitchen enabled him to discern the gold glint of her hair and the pretty shape of her mouth. But it was dim enough that his other senses started to work a little harder. He heard the ragged sound of her breath, and when he cupped her cheek, the pulse in her neck thrummed against the outside of his hand.

Don't let it get too intimate, he reminded himself as he felt another of her little shivers. "I promise you have nothing to be afraid of."

"I know. I'm not afraid of you." She went on tiptoe and her warm breath bathed his lips.

His own shiver rolled down his spine, and he forgot all about promises and concerns and the past and the future.

But he remembered *slow.* So he fitted his mouth to hers with tender care. He pressed against her soft lips and then traced their curves with the tip of his tongue. Under his hands, he felt her body quiver and he traced her lips again, feeling a little purr starting deep in her chest.

His hand moved to cup the back of her head and he slanted his mouth. She drew in a breath and his tongue found entry. He was slow and tender with that, too, gentle strokes and little laps along the insides of her lips.

Against his body, beneath his hands, her skin went hot, but he didn't allow himself to move them. Instead, he focused on her mouth, the silky heat inside, the velvety texture of her tongue. When she pressed closer and twisted against his chest, he could feel the hard nubs of her nipples pushing against him. He wanted to draw up her shirt, draw away her bra, draw those hard points into his mouth and suck and lave and bite....

But he didn't.

He kept up the slow rhythm of the kiss, the sure penetration and retreat of his tongue, even as he felt her muscles humming beneath his hands. The first time her tongue ventured into his mouth and touched the point of his, his half-hard erection leapt to full attention.

He groaned as her pelvis crowded his and she pressed against the long ache. His fingers dropped hers and he slid his hand beneath her shirt. He felt her goose bumps against his fingertips, and he smiled against her mouth. "Ticklish?" he whispered, lifting his head.

Her eyes tightly closed, she shook her head. "Sensitive."

Oh, yeah. That sounded good. It felt even better as he put both hands on her slender rib cage, then moved up his palms to cup her breasts. He groaned. "You're braless. I didn't know you weren't wearing a bra today."

Her nipples were already tight, hard buds. She pressed them against him and pressed her mouth once more to his.

The invitation was clear. He thrust into her mouth again with his tongue, harder, surer, more intent on tasting her. His fingertips circled her sweet little nipples, then moved in to pluck at them with gentle pinches. She made soft sounds from deep in her throat and pressed her hips harder against his body.

Without thinking first, he grabbed the hem of her shirt and yanked it over her head. The move broke their kiss. One look at her surprised face and he thought he'd broken the mood.

Damn it, Jamison. It was supposed to be as far as Linda wants it and no further.

He stepped away. "I'm sorry. I..." His words died off as she stepped closer. She yanked the T-shirt from him and dropped it to the floor, then she lifted his hands toward her nakedness. "Cover me, Emmett."

Oh, God. He wanted to, he had to, he did, whirling her so that her back was to the wall and he could lean against her, his hips flush to hers, his palms cupping her warm breasts, his mouth covering hers, too, making it his.

He plucked her nipples into tight knots and then left her mouth to lean down and taste them, too, sucking them into his mouth with a soft rhythm that made her breathing more ragged. Her fingers slid into his hair, holding him to her.

She tasted so good. He drew his nose against her smooth skin on the way to her other breast, breathing her into his body. Sunshine and flowers and now that creamy sweet smell of her arousal. With his teeth, he tugged lightly on her nipple, distracting her from the direction of his hands as they moved into new territory.

But still, her stomach sucked deep as his fingers slid beneath the waistband of her shorts. "Emmett," she said, her voice breaking a little. "Oh, Emmett."

It wasn't an oh-Emmett-stop "Oh, Emmett," he was certain of that, and he returned to kissing her mouth as he went back to touching the hot, satiny skin of her belly and then the soft curls below. She moaned when his fingertips neared the petals of her sex, and he slid them right into the wet heat waiting for him there.

They both froze, Emmett groaning at the absolute, sweet, sublime pleasure he found in that evidence of her arousal. It turned him on so fast, with so much power, that he thought he might lose it right then and there. She breathed against his ear, hot and heavy, and when he moved his fingers deeper he thought she didn't breathe at all.

His hand flexed, snapping the button at her waist, which eased his access. "I have to touch more of you," he murmured. Pressing his cheek hard against hers, he inserted another finger inside the tight sheath of her body.

She shuddered. "Please, Emmett." Her body was trembling, quivers racking her as he gently withdrew and pushed inside her again. "Please."

Heat was rolling up the back of his thighs, heat was rolling from his neck to his spine, ready to converge between his thighs. He didn't think he could put a lid on the upcoming explosion.

And he didn't care.

"It's time for bed, sweetheart," he said. "It's time to get you naked and get you to a bed."

She nodded. "Yes. Please." But she tightened on his finger as he tried to draw it away.

Which only ratcheted his own desire higher. "Sweetheart, let go. Just for a moment or two. Then I promise I'll fill you with everything I have."

Her eyes were dark, dark pools, the pupils almost as wide as the irises. "And I want everything you have," she said. *"Everything."*

It should have scared him. "I promise." That should have scared him more. But he was too busy turning her toward the bedrooms. His? Hers?

Hers was closer. He put his arm around her shoulders to direct her there, but then remembered. *Condoms, idiot. You can't be inside her without a condom.*

"Hang on," he muttered, turning back toward the bathroom. He had some in the shaving kit he'd stashed in one of the cabinets.

But she wouldn't let him go. Instead, she caught her fingers in the belt loop at the back of his jeans. He glanced back.

"Hanging on," she said.

It made him grin, and he towed her the few feet necessary to the bathroom. He flipped on the light, blinking against the harsh fluorescence. It took only a moment to locate a handful of foil-wrapped packets, then he turned toward Linda. "All—" His voice died.

She was pale, her eyes tightly closed.

"Linda?" he said.

A tear leaked from between a set of brown lashes.

He swallowed. "Linda? What's wrong?" How had he screwed up? What had happened to give her that expression of acute pain? "What have I done wrong?"

Another tear rolled down her cheek. "Not you. Not you." It seemed even hard for her to speak. "Headache. Bad headache."

The knot in his stomach eased. _He_ hadn't hurt her. With gentle hands, he brushed her hair away from her face. "What can I do?"

She made a vague gesture. "The light. Help me get away from the light."

He flipped it off immediately, but could see that it didn't mean an instant end to her pain. She swayed on her feet, and he lifted her into his arms.

Secret agent accountant, tough girl Linda Faraday didn't balk. Instead, she whimpered.

That empty place in Emmett's chest ached like hell. He strode into her bedroom to place her gently between the sheets, then stripped her of her sandals and shorts and drew the sheet over her panty-clad body. She clutched at his hand and whispered something.

"What is it, sweetheart?" He leaned close enough to

her mouth to smell the toothpaste on her breath. She'd tasted like that, too—minty and so damn sweet.

"Pills," she mumbled. "In the medicine cabinet."

He was back with them and a glass of water before another tear had escaped her. With his arm around her back, he shook one out of the bottle and placed it between her lips. She sipped at the water with her eyes closed.

"The light," she whispered again.

"It's off in here, sweetheart. The room is nice and dark."

"It was the light…not you." Her eyes half opened. "You didn't hurt me."

"I know. And I won't." He eased her back onto the pillow.

She reached out for him again. "Emmett!"

He met her seeking fingers with his. "I'm right here. Right here."

"Stay with me, Emmett."

He didn't hesitate. He couldn't. Not when she was still leaking those silent tears. Not when she looked so fragile and defenseless. It was the FBI agent in him, the protector who couldn't walk away from any defenseless creature.

It was impersonal, really. Not intimate.

She insisted he get beneath the sheets with her. That meant he had to slip out of shoes and jeans and slide in wearing only his boxers and his T-shirt. Linda turned on her side and tucked her cute little butt into the cradle of his hips.

She didn't seem to notice the hardness already waiting there.

It noticed *her,* all right, but he ignored the aching

inconvenience and curled his arm around her waist. She let out a sound, half whimper, half sigh.

That damn emptiness in his chest ached harder than his erection.

But he ignored that, too, and stared into the darkness, strands of her flower-fragrant hair beneath his cheek. He hadn't made it into her body, but something about being curved around it was almost more…

No, God, no. It wasn't *intimate*.

Her breathing settled into the rhythm of sleep. His shoulders relaxed. Good, he thought, her pain was lessening.

But he had a feeling that his was just beginning. His erection twitched against her rounded backside.

It was going to be a long night, but he knew he wouldn't leave her.

At least, not tonight.

Emmett couldn't see clearly. He didn't wear glasses, but it was as if he did and he'd lost them. The light was dim as well, and he squinted as he felt his way along the maze of corridors. The sound of his heart was thumping in his ears and his mouth was dry. He was that afraid.

Not afraid for himself. He had his gun in his hand and he could fire it if he had to. Emmett was afraid he'd find no one to fire at.

He was afraid he was going to be too late.

For what? He couldn't quite remember but the anxiety of it was pressing on him, constricting his lungs so that he couldn't take in enough air. The ragged sound of his shallow breaths joined the pound of his heartbeat, a syncopated rhythm of dark, oppressive dread.

Where was she?

The thought slithered through his brain like a snake. *Where was she?*

Around the next corner, he smelled it. Terror and death and blood. Stale blood.

Oh, God. Oh, God, he was too late.

He broke into a run, lurching from side to side against the walls that he couldn't see. His shoulder slammed one side, his gun hand the other, as he rushed closer to the sickening smells that most people would flee from instinctively. Emmett, though, was forced to go forward because that was what he did, that was his job.

Go to the terror, the blood. Find the body because the smells told him there wouldn't be anything happy at the end of this trail.

Another corner, and he found himself in an empty room. A figure stepped out of the shadows. Emmett jerked his gun toward it.

"Christopher!" It was his brother. His big brother. Dead Christopher. "What are you doing here?"

The ghost that was Christopher didn't answer. Instead, he held out a cassette tape.

"I don't want it," Emmett said. "I don't want that."

Christopher shook the tape, insisting.

"No," Emmett said, backing off. "I don't want that. I want her. Where is she?" He tried remembering who *she* was, but it wouldn't come to him.

Then the tape was in his hand, and Christopher was holding out something else now—a small cassette player. He wanted Emmett to play the tape, that was clear, but Emmett wouldn't. He couldn't.

Christopher grabbed the tape from Emmett's hand and slapped it into the player. Horrified, Emmett could only watch as his brother's thumb hovered over the buttons. Then he found his voice again.

"Don't play it!" he yelled out. "Don't play the tape! Don't play the tape!"

"Emmett." A hand was on his shoulder, jostling him. "Emmett, wake up."

It was dark like before. He couldn't see like before. But then he was jostled again and he opened his eyes. It was still night, but unlike a few moments ago now he could easily make out his surroundings. He was in a different room, with a dresser and a mirror and a bed and a…woman.

He was in bed with a woman. Linda.

With a groan, he rolled onto his back. "I'm sorry." He threw an arm over his eyes. "I'm sorry I woke you up. How are you feeling?"

"Better. A little fuzzy, but better. The pills do that to me. How are *you* feeling? You were yelling in your sleep."

"A dream," he muttered.

"A *bad* dream." She smoothed his hair as if he were a child.

Embarrassed, he made to roll off the bed. "I'll get out of here and let you get a good night's rest."

She caught his elbow. "Let me apologize first."

"What?" That was his line.

"I'm sorry about…earlier. The headaches still hit me sometimes."

"I know. Your doctors told me to expect them."

"Yes, well, I'm sorry nevertheless."

"Not necessary." He rolled off the bed until he was on his feet, more than half a mattress away from her. She was sitting up, the sheet pressed to her chest, her hair a long fall of lightness over her bare shoulders. The dream still clutched at him, as well as the humiliation that he'd been caught crying out in his sleep. "Good night."

"Emmett…" Her hair swished as she shook her head. "Let me just say one more time that…that I'm sorry I'm such a failure."

"What?" He stepped forward, his knees bumping the side of the bed. "What are you talking about now?"

"I thought I could be a real woman tonight." Her voice lowered to a whisper. "Instead, I get a screaming headache and then I send you into a screaming nightmare."

Oh, no. No. "My dreams have nothing to do with you."

She made a little noise, and he replayed what he'd said, realizing too late how it sounded.

"That didn't come out right." He sat down on the mattress and found himself reaching for her hand. "It's not easy for me to admit, but it—it was a nightmare. A nightmare that I've had more than once. That I have often. It's not your fault."

She frowned. "But why is that hard for you to admit? Don't you think you're entitled to your demons?"

"I—" He sighed. "I suppose I don't want them to feel entitled to *me*."

She squeezed his fingers. "I always heard you macho FBI men couldn't admit to being mortal like the rest of us. But everyone has bad dreams, Emmett. It doesn't mean you're weak. Now, weak…weak is me."

"Weak? No."

"Incomplete, then. Not all here. Wimpy."

"Linda." Emmett moved closer to her on the bed so that he could touch her face. He tucked her hair behind her ear. "You can't believe that. The fact is, you astonish me with your strength and bravery."

She made another little sound, a disbelieving one.

"Really," he said. "It's funny, I've been around more than my share of hardened male warriors over the years, but it's women who bowl me over with their fortitude and courage every time."

"That's nice of you to say, but—"

"I'm not just saying it." He found her hand again. "I know what I'm talking about. What I dreamed about tonight—my nightmare—is about another young woman whom I admire."

"Who is she?"

"Was. Who she was. She was the last case I worked before I went on leave from the FBI. Her name was Jessica Chandler." He heard the words come out of his mouth and wished them back too late. That case, Jessica herself, was never far from this thoughts. But bringing it up wasn't going to lay any of the ghosts to rest. It was better to keep the thoughts and the ghosts inside himself, where they couldn't bother anyone else's sleep.

"Tell me about her," Linda said.

"No." He hadn't spoken of Jessica to anyone since the investigation ended. And before that, while it was ongoing, he had *listened* to what others had to say about her, letting her mother Leanne and her father John tell him every detail they wanted to relate. He knew her favorite color, her favorite stuffed animal, her favorite hymn. Her little sister shared the name of the first boy who'd ever kissed her. Her older brother told him about the time she'd scratched the family car and he'd covered for her.

Emmett had gotten to know Jessica through the eyes

of those who had loved her most. "It's not a bedtime story," he said. "I shouldn't have mentioned it."

"But you did," Linda pointed out. "Maybe you need to talk about her."

"No." He only needed to bury the details of that case deeper inside himself. Then maybe he could sleep without the terrible dreams. Maybe then he could begin to forget the terrible memories.

"Emmett—"

"She was only eighteen," he heard himself tell Linda, the words bursting out. "Only eighteen years old!"

"Tell me about her," she whispered. "It's all right. I want you to tell me about her."

Despite his wishes, the outrage, the despair, the utter sense of futility that always overcame him at the thought of Jessica Chandler swept through him. Maybe it was because of the recent nightmare, maybe it was because of Linda's sympathetic, soft voice, but this time the barriers he'd erected months ago to wall the pain inside him didn't hold. He had to let it out.

He closed his eyes, squeezing them tight. "She was on her way home from her part-time job. She stopped at the mailbox at the end of her long rural lane. Her brother found her car there less than half an hour later. The door was open, her purse was on the passenger seat, but Jessica was nowhere to be found."

"Kidnapped."

He nodded, his eyes still closed. "That's what brought the FBI in. A beautiful young woman abducted—the situation is chilling. It's hard to have much hope. But her family did. A most remarkable family. They believed in Jessica and her ability to overcome the odds."

Linda stroked the top of his hand with her free fingers. "You got to know her family."

"Yes. Know them, and through them know Jessica. When her kidnapper started calling, I almost began to believe she'd make it out of her nightmare, too." He'd been at the Chandler house 24/7, waiting with her parents and siblings for the phone to ring. From them, he'd learned what a close, loving family could be like and he'd wanted, with increasing desperation, to bring about the happy ending to their appalling ordeal.

"The kidnapper liked to play games with us, though. No straight answers, no putting Jessica on the phone, just enough information for us to know that he did, indeed, have her. He never slipped up by staying long enough on the phone for us to pinpoint his location." Jason had been like that when he held Lily Fortune. In both situations, the too-short, too-taunting calls had eaten at Emmett from the inside out.

"But you did find him?"

"Later. After we recovered Jessica." Emmett opened his eyes. It was edging toward dawn now, and the room was taking on a pearly tone. It had been dawn when the last call from Jessica's abductor had come. His stomach burned with the memory of it. "After a solid week of those teasing phone calls, he gave us GPS coordinates. We found Jessica where he said we would—only she wasn't alive and waiting for us. She was three feet below, in a shallow grave where he'd placed her after killing her two days earlier."

Linda didn't jerk, she didn't cry out, she didn't break away. Instead, she moved in toward Emmett, wrapping her arms around him. She tucked her head in the curve of his neck and shoulder. His cheek found its way against her silky hair. He placed his hands on her warm, sleek back.

There was more, and it was worse, but the walls inside of him were gone and he couldn't keep these words in, either. "She was buried with a cassette tape. On one side he'd recorded— Never mind. On the other, he'd let her tape a final message to her family and friends."

Linda held him tighter.

"It was the most loving last words you could imagine. She asked them not to think of her in the final hours of her life but in all the ones that had come before. Christmases, birthdays, the happy every days that they had shared. Then she sang. She sang the old Simon and Garfunkel song 'Feelin' Groovy.' Can you imagine?" His voice broke, surprising him. He cleared it. "By all reports, she had a terrible voice and could never stay on key, but everyone will tell you that in that recording she sounds like an angel."

His voice broke again. "Just like an angel singing 'Feelin' Groovy.' I heard it myself."

"Oh, Emmett. She must have been quite a young woman."

"I told you. Brave and strong. Not being able to save such a bright, shining star sent me to a very dark place." His body had retreated to a cabin in New Mexico, but his spirit had already been nearly extinguished by layers of blackness and despair. "You've shed some light for me, though."

She lifted her face and scooted back to look at him. "Me?"

He nodded. "I've had the tendency to see the world in shades of black and white. Loser, winner, victim, criminal—"

"Dead, alive."

"And asleep, awake."

Holding the sheet against her chest, she tilted her head. "But I've made you see it's not so simple as that."

He agreed. "You've made me see it's not as simple as that. You're alive and well. Fighting back. Fighting to get your life back. And I know you will."

The room was even brighter now, the pearly gray light taking on the rose and yellow tones of a Texas dawn. Linda looked like the sunrise, with her golden yellow hair and soft pink skin. He could look at her all day, he thought. Because she was bringing daylight into the unrelenting night that had been his existence.

"Your bravery, your fortitude make me believe in goodness again. That it can win."

She was in his arms then, in a flurry of warm skin and crispy sheets. He held her against him, half smiling at the strength of her arms as she squeezed him.

"I think that's the nicest thing anyone has ever said to me," Linda whispered against his neck.

It was the nicest thing anyone had ever done for him, Emmett thought. She'd made him feel almost human again. A man. In the last few months, he'd been trapped in the darkness during the daylight hours just as surely as he was trapped in it during his nightmares. He'd been as much of a ghost as those who peopled his dreams.

But Linda had brought him back to life.

Beneath his cheek, the silky strands of her hair were wet. He touched them as she lifted her head. "I'm sorry," he said. "You're crying."

"It's all right." Her fingers brushed his face. "You are, too."

Chapter 8

Linda saw a disbelieving expression cross Emmett's face as he reached up a hand to feel his tears. She could kick herself for having told him he was crying; no man would appreciate hearing that. But as sometimes had happened since her recovery, her mouth had bypassed a brain check. However, he'd sideswiped her, too, with his talk of strength and bravery.

She almost believed him.

He dried his cheek with the back of his hand. "I don't know whether to hide my face," he said, his voice hoarse, "or kiss yours."

He was beautiful, rumpled and rough and male, looking dark and dangerously sexy in their nest of white sheets. There was something about this hard man revealing glimpses of his soft heart that made her eyes sting again.

His hand reached out to catch the falling tear, and

she turned her cheek into his warm palm to brush her mouth against his fingers. "Kissing sounds good to me," she whispered.

He lifted her chin and pressed his lips to hers, soft as a butterfly. Then his hand moved to cup her bare breast, again, soft as a butterfly. She looked down, surprised by her nakedness. In the midst of their conversation, the covers had slipped and she'd been unaware of it. That happened to her sometimes, too—with her head so busy taking in one thing, she could easily lose track of another.

But now her focus honed in on this. Mesmerized, she watched his big hand on her soft skin, his thumb bumping over the hardening crest of her nipple. The touch affected her twofold—the sight of his darker skin against her pale flesh was almost as arousing as the rub of his calloused fingers against her sensitive nerve endings.

"You'll need to keep breathing, sweetheart," Emmett said.

Her eyes lifted to his. His gaze burned, that yellow flame brightening the green irises like the sun rising outside this very room. She yearned for him, her skin flushing hot as she realized how very, very much she yearned for him.

"I'm not sure I remember how," she whispered, and she knew he knew she wasn't talking about breathing.

With gentle hands he pushed her back against the pillows. He stripped off his T-shirt and then came over her, his bare chest against hers. "You let me worry about that. I'll jog your memory anytime I think you need it, okay?"

She hardly heard him, lost in the wonder of his hard, naked muscles against her. "Okay," she said, and wiggled so that her nipples brushed against him.

He groaned.

"Does that hurt?" she asked, all innocence. "Did I get it wrong already?"

"Tease." His mouth descended, brushing hers. "But two can play that game."

And oh, he played it well. He teased her, all right, pressing just the lightest of kisses against her mouth, one, then two, then lifting on three so that she tried to follow his mouth to make the kisses longer, deeper, *more.* But that tempting mouth was already on the move, sliding down her neck, licking a hot path from behind her ear to her collarbone to the shallow valley between her breasts.

He plumped one with his hand, and she held her breath, waiting for the delicious heat of his mouth, but instead he gently brushed his stubbled cheek against her hard nipple, the prickly sensation raising goose bumps from her forehead to her feet. As he moved to the other breast, her muscles tensed. She wanted his mouth there. She wanted that ticklish tantalizing of his beard. She wanted *more.*

Her gaze trained on his face, she waited to see what he would do next. Hovering over her left nipple, his tongue reached out.

He glanced at her, then lifted his head.

She wanted to scream or cry or beg. *Please.*

He must have known. A little smile played over his mouth. "I think it's time for one of those little memory jogs. You can ask for what you want, sweetheart. As a matter of fact, it's a requirement."

"Words…" Linda swallowed. "Words aren't always easy to come by."

"Then show me."

She figured he already knew. She figured this was

more of that teasing he wanted to treat her to, but he'd said it was a requirement, and she didn't want to take the chance of getting anything wrong. So she slid her fingers into the short strands of his hair and brought his lips to her breast.

They opened over her nipple and sucked it into the wet heat of his mouth. Linda cried out. "Yes," she heard herself say. "Yes, yes, yes."

He sucked at the other one, too, making them both hard and wet and so sensitive that her body arched off the bed as he drew his thumbs over the tips. "Now is when I take your panties off," he said. "Now is when I get to see all of you."

Her hips fit perfectly between his palms. He drew his hands over their curves, taking her underwear with them.

Struck by a sudden bout of modesty, she brought her naked legs tightly together. The sun had risen and the room was morning-bright. "I've only done this in the dark," she said, not sure why she was feeling so nervous again.

His big hand sat warmly on her upper thigh. "Then I'll be your first daylight man."

Daylight man. Dark and troubled Emmett, who had so many of his own demons, had come into her life to help her. And here he was again. Her daylight man. Maybe they could bring the sun to each other.

She parted her legs and opened her arms. "Please."

He slipped out of his boxers, rolled on a condom and then came between her thighs. Closing her eyes, she reveled in his heat, his weight, the exquisite feel of his body, so male and hard against hers.

"Memory jog," he said against her mouth. "Open your thighs wider, sweetheart, and tilt your hips."

"Oh." His erection slid against her sensitive flesh, the way slickened by her arousal. He came a little way inside her and held there, his weight balanced on his elbows.

She wiggled her bottom a little, but he didn't make a move. "Memory jog," she said, her voice sounding tight and a bit desperate. "Don't stop now."

He smiled down at her. "I'm just enjoying the view. Your eyes are so blue right now. Your cheeks are flushed and your mouth and your nipples are the exact same shade of raspberry." He leaned lower to brush his tongue along her bottom lip. "Delicious."

She grabbed his head and brought him down for a proper kiss. He let her arrange the alignment of their mouths but then took over again, his tongue entering her even as that other part of him pushed inside.

Linda whimpered, her body quivering around his slow and steady penetration. *Good,* she thought to herself. *So good.*

He pulled his hips back, and then did it again, opening her to him with another sure and patient push. Linda felt her skin flush hotter, and her fingers bit into his scalp. He grunted, his body grinding against hers. His mouth lifted and he whispered in her ear, his breath hot against the sensitive shell.

"You remember this now, right? You remember how we try to hold out as long as we can, teasing each other, letting the tension build?"

She nodded her head, even though she didn't think it had ever been like now for her before. How could it have been, when Emmett had never before been in her arms, in her body, his heavy erection sliding in and out of her, touching her inside, pulling against the little knot of nerves at the apex of her sex?

He rolled, and she found herself on top of him. It had never been like this, for sure it had never been like this, because there was sunlight in the room and sunlight added another layer of heat to her skin. It streamed in one of the windows, washing over Emmett's torso and washing over hers as she sat up on her knees. He covered her breasts with his big hands, and his hips arched into hers.

It had never been like this, because every thrust tightened her arousal and took it higher, to a place she'd never seen before. It was a wild rainbow of colors that she saw behind her closed eyelids as she tried to keep herself on that fine knifelike edge of erotic tension.

She heard herself whimper because it was so good, too good, and she didn't know what the next step was, how to take it, what would happen when she fell.

"Linda."

Her eyes opened, and Emmett was looking up at her, his features hardened by the same passion she was feeling. He drew one hand from her breast, over her stomach, to the place they were joined.

"Memory jog," he said, touching her there. "It's time to come."

His fingers pressed again, rolled, and she did fall, her body shuddering around his. It was a free fall of delight through the rainbow, only made brighter, sweeter by the guttural sounds of Emmett's own climax.

As she touched back down, she collapsed onto his body. His arms came around her.

Her daylight man.

And in the sunshine of that thought, she slept.

On his way out the door for his morning coffee, Jason stuffed his pockets with some of the ransom cash from the Lily Fortune kidnapping. One of his bigger problems in this game of cat and mouse he was playing with his brother was that he had to lug the damn money around. He couldn't get a safe-deposit box in a bank, even using one of his fake IDs, because it might mean getting caught on a surveillance camera. It also would mean he couldn't take off the instant it suited him. And he wanted twenty-four-hour access to his money.

After picking up the two million from the ransom drop, he'd sped away from the site and sped into a collision with a farmer's daughter and her load of eggs. That unwelcome snag was smoothed out, though, when a Lexus had happened upon the scene. Jason had carjacked the suit who was driving and then taken off in his luxury automobile, leaving the egg woman ducttaped to the dude in Armani. Jason and his duffel bags of money had looked good in that borrowed sedan, but he'd been forced to dump it. No doubt at some point, the suit would have freed himself and called it in as stolen.

At the outskirts of the next little town, he'd left the Lexus behind and then paid cash for a wreck from some wiry old man who only spoke Spanish. Since the guy had met him at his front door with a shotgun, Jason figured he wouldn't be much friendlier to any cops that came around. So he thought it was semisafe to leave one of the duffels stuffed in the trunk of the rusted Buick, where the spare was supposed to sit.

The other he had been forced to carry around with him. The rent-by-the-week motel room he'd found in the next little town after that had had flimsy locks on the doors and the kind of clientele who didn't look you in the eye. His new place was better, though. He felt okay about leaving for short periods of time with the

Do Not Disturb sign on the door and the duffel stashed in the space behind the TV in the cabinet that held it.

Two duffel bags worth two million in cash shouldn't seem like an inconvenience, but they were. Just something else to blame on straight-arrow Emmett.

Jason walked a few blocks for his coffee, passing a convenience store and a Starbucks that he'd already visited on other mornings. People tended to remember regulars, and he wanted to be as unmemorable as possible.

At the next location of the ubiquitous chain, he shuffled into the line of others waiting for their morning fix. A woman in a tailored business dress and pumps glanced back at him, then smiled and nodded toward the others ahead. "Every morning I think that I should save the almost four bucks and the hassle of getting up an extra fifteen minutes early to stand in this line, and every morning I get up and do it all over again."

Jason smiled at her. Women liked him, they always had. "I know what you mean. It makes it a little easier when you own a substantial chunk of stock in the company, though."

Her brown eyes widened. "Is that right?"

He nodded to affirm the lie. "With every cup I order, I feel as if I'm paying myself."

She was at the front of the line now, so he walked up to the counter with her. "I'll be buying for both of us," he told the clerk behind the cash register. The businesswoman gave him another smile. "What'll you have?" he asked her.

They took their coffees to one of the small round tables. She said she had a little time before she had to be at her desk. Jason thought appearing as part of a couple would throw off anyone who might come around looking for him. Besides, the woman was pretty and he hadn't had a pretty woman to talk to since he'd killed that bitch Melissa.

"So what is it you do?" the woman asked. Her name was Joanne and she was an architect.

"I'm a private eye," Jason told her.

"You're kidding!" Joanne had gullible blue eyes.

"Nope." After all, he *was* detecting. "I'm working on a case right now involving a missing person." He couldn't leave the country until he found his brother Emmett and neutralized him.

"Fascinating. Just fascinating."

The way Joanne the architect was looking at him made him think the private-eye line was a damn good one. Wherever he ended up, Mexico, or Belize, or Brazil, he was going to have some cards made up. Jason Jamison—no. He thought of the name on his new passport, Francis Dixon. He'd bought one under Jordan Collins first, but it had reminded him, unpleasantly, of his law-and-order cousin, Collin Jamison, so he'd put out the cash for another. Frank Dixon, private detective. The chicks would love it, would love *him*.

The chick across the table took another sip of her coffee. "What made you choose that line of work?"

Jason let his expression turn sad and his gaze grow distant. "My wife… My wife was murdered." Not far from the truth, except that Melissa was merely posing as his spouse. And he had killed her.

Joanne gasped, then reached her hand across the table to cover his. "My God. I'm so sorry."

He turned his hand and grasped her fingers. God, this line was a babe magnet! Maybe he should get himself a computer before he headed out of the country and use it to write a book. *The Best Love Lies.* Or *Fib Your*

Way into the Sack. "The experience was wrenching, needless to say. Now I'm committed to…" Getting back at his sanctimonious little brother. "…justice for all."

Emmett would pay.

Joanne was staring at him as if he were a sensitive Tom Hanks and a bad boy Colin Farrell rolled into one. "How do you go about it, though? Is it like the television shows or is it more mundane than that? A lot of computer work, I suppose."

He shrugged. "Sometimes. But mostly it's asking the right questions of the right people." His only real difficulty had been to fake reasons for asking the questions he needed the answers to. And that he couldn't ask them in person. "The man whose trail I'm on had been staying at an inn in the little town of Red Rock. But he checked out a couple of weeks ago."

It pissed Jason off that he hadn't considered the possibility that Emmett would leave the area around the Fortune ranch. His little brother had toadied up to Ryan while the old goat was dying, and Jason had just assumed he'd stick around to shine the apples of the weeping widow, Lily. But once the old man had kicked the bucket, Emmett had kicked the Red Rock dust off his shoes.

Maybe because he'd gotten what he'd wanted—that nice inheritance from Ryan. It would surprise Jason to find out that his younger brother was thinking of Number One for once, but maybe that was why he'd left town. Whatever the reason, it had put a crimp in Jason's plans. He'd loved the idea of Emmett holed up in the Corner Inn in downtown Hickville, aka Red Rock, wondering when Jason was going to appear on his doorstep.

It was what he'd assumed Emmett was doing, staying

holed up, and it had made Jason feel all happy inside to know his brother was waiting for the other shoe to drop. He'd spent several nights in the motel with a case of beer, toasting the idea.

"So how are you going to find this missing person now?"

Jason blinked, then looked at pretty Joanne. He'd forgotten what she'd asked. "Excuse me?"

"I said, how are you going to find your missing person?"

"Ah. That's where the right questions and the right person comes in. When I realized my target had checked out of the inn, I called to see if he'd left a forwarding address."

"They just give out that kind of information over the phone?" Joanne looked as if the thought was scandalous.

"I said I was holding a delivery for him from Washington, D.C. Mention the capital and everyone assumes it's important."

"So you know where to find this man now?"

He wished. "Nothing is ever quite that easy, I'm afraid. They told me he had left a forwarding address, but it turns out to be a business." A business that Jason knew well. The Fortune TX, Ltd. headquarters. On Kingston Street, in honor of that miserly bastard who hadn't had the kindness to help out Jason's grandfather, Farley, all those years ago. Months ago Jason had worked in that very office building, planning to use his business know-how and wily street smarts to bring financial and personal ruin down on Kingston's son Ryan.

"So was it a ruse? You know, to throw people looking for him off the trail?" Joanne asked.

"No, he has some ties to that business. So I'm guessing he'll show up there sooner or later. I'll stake the place out, pick up his scent. He's in San Antonio, and now so am I. I'll find him."

Emmett drifted out of a deep sleep. It struck him as odd, that deep sleep, because he didn't sleep well as a general rule. Hadn't for years. His eyes opened and he took in several unusual things at once: the bright light indicated it was well into morning; there was a sheet-covered lump next to him; he was wearing a smile on his face.

That scared the hell out of him. He wiped his face with his hands to erase the expression, even as he remembered what he'd been doing before dropping into that deep sleep. The sex had been great, no doubt about it, but it was nothing to smile about. He had to be careful not to give Linda the wrong idea.

He wasn't going to be sticking around.

The lump moved, stretched. Beneath the sheet, a hand flung out and landed on his bare chest. The lump froze. Then the hand patted the flesh it had found, as if trying to figure out what it was by touch. Her pinkie encountered his nipple.

The sheet whipped over Linda's head and she stared at Emmett, her hair a rumpled mass of gold.

He didn't know why that made him want to smile again. "Memory jog," he said to her confused face. "We—" How to put this without using a word as misleading as *love* or one as crass as *sex?* "—now have carnal knowledge of each other."

She gripped the edge of the sheet between her fists and held it tightly to her throat. "'Carnal knowledge'?"

His desire to smile died. Anxiety put its cold hand

on the back of his neck. He couldn't read the expression on Linda's face, and he wasn't even sure what he wanted her to feel. Satisfied, yes. But beyond that, he didn't know. He shouldn't have told her so much about himself in those dark hours of early, early morning. Jessica Chandler. The darkness that was inside of him. Linda was bound to read more into what they'd done together after what he'd revealed to her.

She sat up, still clutching the sheet over the body parts that he'd so enjoyed just a few hours before. Her mouth opened, and he braced himself for whatever morning-after comment she might make.

"Does that mean you'll make the coffee while I take a shower?"

Shaking his head, Emmett trudged off to the kitchen. He was smiling again, damn it. But there he'd been, all poised to deliver a we-have-no-future speech, and she'd robbed him of the opportunity by demanding nothing more than caffeine in liquid form.

Lily Fortune had been right. Linda apparently wasn't interested in his staying power.

Within thirty minutes, it was like any other morning that had gone on before at the guest house. He and Linda were both sitting at the kitchen table, sipping coffee and sharing the newspaper. Emmett told himself he was glad of it, of course, but wasn't it somewhat odd? It seemed damned odd to him, but that could be because he never had stuck around long enough to enjoy breakfast with his occasional one-night stands.

His fingers crumpled the edges of the sports section he was holding open. Was that what she'd expected from him? A one-night stand?

She turned the page of the section she was reading and let out a little sigh.

He glanced over at her. She looked daisy-fresh, despite the little frown turning down her mouth. "What's the sigh for?" he asked. "What're you thinking about?"

Her little frown turned to a grimace. "The future."

His stomach jumped. Damn it! See? He'd been right. He should have stayed away from her, because now she was linking the two of them together in a way he'd never intended.

He cleared his throat. They would have to have this conversation sometime, he supposed. "What about the future?"

She tapped the newspaper with her forefinger. "My future employment."

He blinked. He'd been certain she was going to want to talk about the nonexistent *them,* but she'd gone ahead and surprised him again. Taking a sip of his coffee, he glanced at what she'd been reading. The classifieds. "No want ads for a secret agent accountants?" he asked.

She shot him a truculent look. "If you keep that up, you're going to pay."

Maybe he already was, he thought. Because with that little pout to her mouth, all he could think about was kissing her again, holding her, smelling her, feeling her tighten around him as she climaxed. He shifted in his chair. "I didn't realize you were eager to restart your career."

"My old career is over. There are several reasons I wouldn't be welcomed back at the Treasury Department. First and foremost, I showed a distinct lack of judgment when I got involved with Cameron Fortune— the subject of an investigation."

Emmett sipped his coffee again to hide his reaction to the other man's name. Frankly, he hated the dead guy's guts. Ryan had told him the kind of man his brother had been, and Emmett was certain that Cameron had seduced a young Linda with an expertise that she couldn't have expected or been prepared for. She'd been young and alone and looking for a family, he remembered her saying, which would certainly have made her only that much more vulnerable to an older man's wiles.

"I don't much like the idea of you going back to work there myself," he heard himself say. Now, where had that come from? He didn't want a say in her future, and he didn't want her expecting he wanted one.

She was looking at him with a puzzled expression on her face.

"For Ricky," he said, as a way to explain himself. "I'm thinking of him." Yeah, sure.

But Linda nodded. "You're right, of course. I have a young son now. A responsibility I take seriously. I need to find a line of work that doesn't risk my health and well-being, and that keeps me available for Ricky when he needs me." She frowned again. "If he ever needs me."

That downturn of her lips had that void in his chest aching again, and he rubbed at the pain. "I hope I'm not getting too personal," he said, as if he hadn't had her nipples in his mouth and her hips in his hands just hours before, "but my understanding was that Ryan provided both you and Ricky with trust funds that should leave you financially more than comfortable for the rest of your lives. You don't need to work."

Maybe it *was* too personal, because she lowered her brows and shot him a narrow-eyed look. "I hope *I'm* not getting too personal, but my understanding is that Ryan left *you* a pile of money, too, and I don't hear you considering sitting on your behind for the rest of your life, Mr. G-Man."

"I…" He hadn't meant to insult her. "I don't think I'm going back to the FBI, as a matter of fact." His brain replayed the admission, because it was the first time it had ever heard the thought. He wasn't going back to the FBI?

"Why?"

I don't know. Why wouldn't I go back to the FBI? "You have to hope when you're an FBI agent," he said slowly. "I've lost most of that. And you have to care. I don't think I care enough anymore."

"Or you care too much," Linda said.

"No." That wasn't true. He didn't want it to be true. "But I'm a lawyer by education, so I'll probably end up getting some fat-cat clients out of the punishments they so richly deserve."

She was already shaking her head. "No, you won't. I don't believe that for a minute."

"No, I won't." He didn't try pretending he didn't appreciate the faith she had in him. "But I'd like to do something involving the law."

Linda quieted, seeming lost in thought. "I have an idea," she said after a few moments.

"An idea for your career?"

"No, for yours."

"Me?" Until a few minutes ago, he hadn't even realized he needed one.

"Now, don't look annoyed," she said. "I'm only thinking of your future."

"I'm not annoyed." Okay, he was. Because she kept yanking the rug from beneath his feet. He'd woken up, worried he was going to have to make clear *they* had no future, and now here she was, figuring out what he should do for the rest of his life. The rest of his life without her. Shouldn't she want more from him than that?

She deserved everything from a man.

"Don't you want to know my idea?" she asked.

"I suppose you're going to tell me anyway."

"Well, you're right about that. But I was thinking about Ryan, and how we both owe him a lot, and I got to thinking about all the other people and charities that he's helped over the years. Lily told me he'd wanted to set up some kind of philanthropic foundation but he ran out of time."

Emmett looked down at his coffee. "A man like Ryan shouldn't have run out of time," he muttered.

"Well, here's how you can help with that," Linda said.

He raised his gaze to hers.

"*You* can set up the foundation. Ryan left the money. It just needs someone who knows his way through the legal channels and who knows Ryan's heart. It would be good work, Emmett, and a way to build on the legacy that Ryan left behind. I'm certain Lily would think it's a great idea."

Good work...and a way to build on the legacy that Ryan left behind.

Emmett couldn't believe how much the notion appealed to him. How right it felt. "That would mean staying here in Texas," he said slowly.

"I suppose." A blush rose up Linda's neck as she stared down at her coffee.

Because it meant they'd be in the same state? Was she thinking of a future for them, after all? Or worrying that *he* was grasping at ways to stay near to her?

Maybe he was, he thought, as another idea mushroomed out of hers. "A foundation like you're suggesting would need its very own secret agent accountant," he said. "Well, not the secret agent part, but definitely an accountant."

Her gaze lifted from her cup to his face. He couldn't read what it said. She opened her mouth and he braced for his worst fear. Which was that? That she'd agree? That she'd disagree?

A fist pounded on the kitchen door. A kid face peered through the window there. Ricky, interrupting the moment.

Thank God, Emmett thought. And, *damn.*

Chapter 9

Less than an hour later, Emmett watched through the kitchen window as Linda passed the soccer ball back and forth to Ricky. The kid was a good player, and Linda was a lousy one, but they both handled the situation with good grace. He took another sip of his coffee. Despite Linda's worries, she was going to be a good mother. She *was* a good mother.

Without even thinking it over, he drew his cell phone from his pocket and punched in a familiar number, but one that he'd called only very rarely in recent years. It was answered by a soft voice, and guilt almost had him hanging up. But his gaze found Ricky and Linda again, and he forced himself to speak.

"Hi, Mom. It's me."

"Emmett! I—I'm so happy to hear from you."

"Not to mention surprised, eh, Mom?" He could see her in the kitchen, making her second pot of morning tea. At Christopher's funeral, he'd vowed to himself to keep in touch more, but somehow he'd allowed himself to drift apart from his parents again.

"Maybe I *am* surprised, but that doesn't take away the pleasure of hearing your voice."

The former Darcy Derosier had been the toast of her small Texas town when his father had wandered in, stricken with amnesia following a car accident. Blake Jamison had been tended to by the Derosier clan and won the heart of its beautiful daughter. She was a gentle yet strong Southern woman, one of those famed steel magnolias. But Emmett knew she was grieving heavily for the loss of both her sons: the murdered Christopher as well as Jason, whose criminality no one could explain or excuse.

"How are you doing, Mom?"

"I'm keeping on keeping on, as your father would say," she told him, a little sigh in her voice. "We started a scholarship in your brother's name at your old high school."

"That's a great idea." He took a breath. "I'm thinking of setting up and running a foundation to benefit Ryan's favorite charities and projects."

"You're going to leave the FBI?"

"Yeah. I guess I am." The more he said it, the more right it sounded. "Do you think that's a bad idea?"

"I don't think you have bad ideas, Emmett. You've always been good at what you do, but naturally I've worried about you being in law enforcement. More now than ever."

Now that she'd lost her other sons. "I've never been injured, Mom."

"I've worried about your emotions, your heart," she answered. "It's a dark business you've been in."

"Yeah." And of course his father would have told her how he'd found Emmett in the Sandia Mountains some months back, trying to drink all his pain away. Emmett could tell her he didn't have a heart, but it wouldn't be a comforting thought. And after last night…let's just say he didn't want to examine the subject too closely.

"So I'll be glad to see you out of the FBI."

"I'm going to find Jason first." Emmett squeezed shut his eyes, wishing he hadn't brought up his brother's name.

"I'll be glad of that, too." His mother's voice had lowered to almost a whisper. "I can't bear the thought of him hurting anyone else."

"It's not your fault, Mom. You know that."

"Then you should know that mothers carry guilt as well as dish it out."

He laughed at that, as she'd meant him to. She was a remarkable woman, his mother. Her hurt went deep, but so did her love. "I'd like you to meet another special mother I know."

Outside, Linda was standing in the sunlight, inspecting Ricky's grubby hand. He'd showed Emmett a minuscule splinter the day before, and it looked as if he was seeking more sympathy from his mom now.

"A special woman or a special mother?" Darcy Jamison asked.

One smart cookie, he thought, with a wry grin. "Both."

"You're talking about the girl, Linda, that Ryan asked you to look after. The one you're staying with."

"She's not a girl. She's all—" *Woman,* he'd been about to say. But his smart-cookie mom would read a wealth of detail into that. "She's older than me, as a matter of fact. And her kid… You'd really like her kid."

"It sounds like you do, as well."

"Yeah. Yeah, I do. Ricky's easy to like. He's ten, a soccer player and a traffic patrol officer and a better speller than I am. He likes his pizza Hawaiian-style and his hands dirty."

His mother laughed. "Now, those last two sound like someone I already know."

Her laughter spread more balm over the wounds of the past few months. Last night Linda had started her own kind of healing, but reconnecting with his mother was helping, too. "You should come for a visit. Lily's still planning that big Fortune family reunion at the end of the month."

"Oh, Emmett. I'm not sure."

"I am. I want you to meet Ricky. He could use a—"

"Grandmother?"

Emmett froze. Was that what he was thinking? If his mother were Ricky's grandmother, then that would make him Ricky's...father. Was he really considering becoming the kid's dad?

The boy burst through the kitchen door just as the question sank into Emmett's brain. Linda followed more slowly behind, but her long legs ate up the distance between them all the same. Emmett backed himself against the refrigerator, staring at her. If he became Ricky's dad, then he became Linda's...husband.

Was that what he was really thinking?

"Emmett?" It was his mother's voice.

He shook his head, trying to regain his focus. "I'm here, Mom."

"What's this little boy's favorite kind of pie?"

"I don't know. Hold on." He thrust the phone toward Ricky. "You have a call, champ."

Ricky turned toward him. "Me?"

"It's regarding pie. And it's my mother, so be polite."

The boy took the phone. "Hello?"

Linda was looking at Emmett. "What's this all about?"

Where this might go between us. Where I can't believe I'm thinking this might go between us.

Yet he was smiling again, and he found himself walking to her, grabbing her chin and turning her face up for his kiss. She made a little startled sound, then whispered fiercely when he lifted his head. "Ricky!"

But the kid had his back to them. Emmett heard him offer up apple and peach pie, but put a definite nix on blueberry. He'd never liked blueberry pie, either. "He's preoccupied at the moment," he told Linda, swooping in for another kiss. "It'll take a few more years for him to be thinking of dessert and kisses at the same time."

Linda backed away. She didn't look mad, just confused. Guess what? He was confused, too. He hadn't felt this optimistic in…maybe his whole life.

How strange was that? Earlier, he had been worried about Linda thinking of forevers; instead, it was he who was thinking of them. He'd told her she'd brought light into his life and, God, it was true.

Ricky held up the phone, grinning. "She says you were not only a lousy speller, but you don't make beds very well, either."

"Let me have that." He whipped the cell out of the kid's hand. "Mom, you shouldn't be telling all my secrets."

She was laughing again. Oh, yeah, there was light everywhere. "He's delightful, Emmett. And I have to work on my peach pies. I haven't made one in years."

"Then you'll have to bring one or two to us here,"

he said. "Ricky is drooling already, just thinking about them."

"What about Linda? What kind of pie does she like?"

He glanced over at her bright blond hair. "Apple," he said with confidence. "She's an apple-pie kind of girl."

"I thought you said she was a woman," his mother chided him, and there was a sly giggle in her voice. "But apple it is. I can't wait to meet her, too."

Their call ended with more good humor and looking-forward-to-seeing-you promises. Emmett flipped his phone closed and found himself humming.

Keeping with the uncommon theme he had going, Emmett called his cousin Collin and made arrangements to meet for lunch in Red Rock. They decided upon Emma's, a popular café and local hangout facing the town square. Typical to them both, they pulled into the parking lot at the same time, twelve minutes early.

Emmett gave the other man's hand a firm shake. "Good to see you, cousin."

Collin did an exaggerated double take. "Who are you and what have you done with my frozen-hearted Fed of a friend?"

"Shut up."

"Seriously. The Emmett I know hasn't smiled since he beat me at Indian wrestling when he was ten."

"As long as you remember I *did* beat you, I'll keep on smiling."

"Hey, then I grew four inches and kicked your butt at every opportunity the next summer until you cried to your mom about it."

They were shown to a table in the shade outside by Emma's very own Emma Mirabeau. When she hurried off to fetch the iced teas they'd ordered, Emmett looked over at his cousin. "I talked to her today," he said.

Collin narrowed his eyes. "Your mother?"

Emmett nodded.

"That's good. She needs to hear from you more often."

"I know. She's actually considering coming to Lily's big reunion now. And bringing pies. A peach pie for Ricky and an apple pie for Linda."

Collin relaxed back in his chair. "Pies, huh? For Ricky and Linda. It all sounds very cozy."

Emma brought their iced teas and took their orders. Collin and Emmett, no surprise, went for the same thing. The big burger platter. They came quickly, a half pound of prime Texas beef and crisp, golden steak fries.

Collin spoke again as Emmett lifted one of the potato wedges to his mouth. "So how cozy is it exactly, Emmett?"

He dropped the fry to take a big gulp from his glass instead. "How's my favorite redheaded medical student?"

"Talking about Lucy won't distract me, buddy."

Emmett took another drink from his glass. "Maybe it's very cozy," he said slowly. "Or heading that way."

Now Collin was smiling. "You're kidding me."

"No. Maybe. I'm not sure." He drummed his fingers against the tabletop. "She…has a way about her that—"

Collin slapped his thigh and grinned. "Ho-ho! The mighty, the morose, oh, how he has fallen."

Emmett scowled. He remembered a time when Collin had been as world-weary as he had always felt. "Hasn't anyone ever told you it's not polite to crow? You didn't see me ho-ho-ing when you were making yourself silly over Lucy."

"Military men never make themselves silly." Collin was still foolishly grinning. "Take that back."

Emmett shook his head. Where had all his cousin's former bitterness disappeared to? Had Lucy brought to Collin the same kind of light that Linda had brought to him? "You have gotten downright clownlike thanks to this love thing, do you know that?"

"Takes one to know one."

"I'm not in love with Linda." Emmett picked up the ketchup bottle. "Don't go that far." He was a protector; they had a powerful sexual attraction. It was only natural that he might be considering taking her under his wing on a more…protracted basis. Maybe something like— but he couldn't even think the *M* word. Not now. Not yet.

Collin appeared to bite the inside of his cheek. "Okay. It's very cozy, but it's not love. Got it."

"I'm regretting inviting you to lunch."

"Why did you?"

Emmett met his cousin's gaze. "Jason. We need to talk about Jason."

"Is there any news?"

"Not beyond that call he made to me a couple of weeks back," Emmett replied. As an Army Ranger for the CIA special ops, Collin was notorious for his ability to understand those he hunted. He understood the way a twisted man's head worked, which was why his request to transfer to Austin as a trainer had happened so quickly. Collin's talents were legendary. "Do you think Jason has fled the country after all?"

"Let's go over again what he told you in that call."

"He seemed angry that I was named in Ryan's will. 'Why should you get any of the Fortune money when it was me who worked so hard for it?' he asked. Then he said, 'Keep looking over your shoulder, Emmett, because I'm coming after you.'"

Repeating the words brought it all back to him. That sense of evil he'd smelled in the air at the sound of his brother's voice. The crazed malevolence in his brother's tone.

He met his cousin's level gaze. "Jason hasn't left the country, has he, Collin?"

Shrugging, the other man watched him carefully. "You're as experienced as I am in this kind of case."

Emmett rolled his shoulders as if he could shift the heavy weight he felt there. "I swore I'd get him. I made a vow to Ryan that I would put a stop to my brother. I've not been making progress."

"Ryan didn't ask for that vow," Collin pointed out. "He asked you to look after Linda and Ricky. You've been seeing to that."

"Still… Not one of us will be free until we have him behind bars. My mother says she's coming to Lily's Fortune family reunion, but you and I both know she won't, not if Jason is still free. And my father… I know he feels more guilt and fear each day."

"And you, Emmett? How do you feel?"

"Like I didn't do enough. Like I should have seen it coming since we were little kids. Jason hated Christopher, hated everything about him, from the Boy Scout badges he earned to the quiet way he cared about others around him." And even though he'd admired Christopher, Emmett had never been close to him, either. The animosity Jason felt had been a looming presence in their household, and Emmett had distanced himself from it by distancing himself from every member of his family.

"No one could predict what Jason would become."

"Yeah. And yet we still believe we should have. Maybe that's what I think I can end by stopping him."

"It's the FBI's job, Emmett."

"I *am* the FBI."

"On leave. And under no obligation to pursue a family member."

"A couple of months ago, both of us were doing just that," Emmett reminded him. "Should I apologize for dragging you into that?"

"Hell, no." Collin flashed him a quick smile. "It's how I found my Lucy, right? But we both are aware that Jason has no scruples. He'll do anything. I don't want to see you get hurt."

"I won't."

"What about Linda and Ricky?"

"Don't you think I've already thought about that? From the very beginning? But my brother has no way of even knowing they exist or that I'm staying at the Armstrongs'. In any case, I take precautions. I never return to the guest house without ensuring I'm not being tailed." But dread was washing over him, and washing away all the optimism he'd felt that morning. He'd made the decision to involve himself with Linda because he'd promised Ryan. He hadn't been using his FBI brain then.

"I should put the brakes on," he muttered.

"With Linda?"

"Jason hangs over me like a dark cloud."

"There goes your happy smile."

"Do you blame me?" Emmett asked. "Would you allow yourself to get close to a woman knowing the ugliness that I do?"

Collin shrugged. "I know I was pleased to see you

talking about your mom, and pies, and cozy situations with a woman and her boy."

Emmett pushed away his plate with his half-eaten hamburger. Cozy didn't seem right, not right now. "I can be that man again, when I get Jason."

"So in the meantime you're just going to sit around, waiting for him to tap you on the shoulder?"

"No." The longer Jason remained free, the more risk there was to the innocents of the world, including Linda and Ricky. "I'm going to think of some way to flush him out."

Collin nodded slowly. "Knowing what we do about your brother, that will work. You can't be too obvious, of course. He'll see through that and then be able to resist the lure. But if you can get yourself in the public eye, some publicity that has to do with good deeds or your new inheritance, or both, that should tweak Jason enough to draw him out of wherever he's hiding."

Emmett drummed his fingers on the tabletop again. "Good deeds…the new inheritance…"

"You have an idea?"

"A glimmer of one." Emmett drained the last of his iced tea.

"What are you going to do about the lady?"

Emmett glanced at Collin. "Who?"

His cousin rolled his eyes. "The one you're cozy with! Damn, man. Have you forgotten already?"

No. He couldn't forget Linda for half a second. Not her incredible silky hair, the tight sheath of her body, the sweet surprise on her face when he stroked her breasts. But he had to back off from her and where they'd been heading until he found Jason. There could be no promises—spoken or unspoken—about the future yet. There'd be no more kisses or coziness or warm mornings in her bed until his brother was behind bars.

Today is Monday.
You made love with Emmett three mornings ago, but he's barely spoken to you since. Don't make a fool of yourself and be too friendly.
Stop using his soap!

Linda looked over the words in her notebook before leaving her bedroom for the kitchen. She sniffed her just-showered forearm and relaxed. It was her usual floral scent, as opposed to the muskier one that had driven her crazy the past couple of days. With Emmett keeping his distance, she couldn't understand why his scent had seemed to surround her—until she realized she'd been lathering up with his bar in the shower.

This morning in the bathroom, she'd remembered to keep her hands off his things. Okay, fine, she'd opened his shampoo and taken a quick whiff of its manly fragrance, but she'd recapped it right away. Temptation wouldn't get the best of her. Not for his shampoo, not for *him*. Even a head-injured person had some pride, and Emmett's hands-off attitude made his position clear.

He didn't want her anymore.

But she wanted coffee, so she squared her shoulders and headed into the kitchen. As usual, he was sitting at the table with a mug and the San Antonio paper.

She gave him her brightest smile and her cheeriest voice. "Good morning!"

He gave her a surly grunt in return. He hadn't shaved and there were shadows beneath his eyes. If he still wasn't so gorgeous, she would have suspected he wasn't sleeping any better than she was.

She squeezed shut her eyes and turned away from him.

"Headache?" he asked.

"What?" She glanced over her shoulder at him.

"You're squinching your eyes. I thought maybe you felt another headache coming on."

Linda thought he hadn't even looked up from his paper. "No, no headache." She didn't want him to guess that what was bothering her was *him.* "A little restless, that's all."

He grunted again. "We haven't been working out."

No, they hadn't. She figured it was because he wanted to keep as far away from her as possible. Somehow, she'd turned him off or done something to turn him away from her. But she wasn't going to worry about it. Didn't she have more important things to think of?

He lifted his mug to his mouth. Beneath his T-shirt, his bicep bunched and she stared at it, fascinated. What would it feel like beneath her cheek, against her mouth? If she traced the curve with her tongue, would his skin heat just as hers was doing right this very instant?

Making love with him had affected her memory, all right. She couldn't seem to forget how fabulous he had felt under her hands and inside her body.

Her daylight man.

"Linda?"

She blinked and noted he'd observed her preoccupation. She was still staring at him. Whirling back to the coffee, she cleared her throat. "What?"

She poured the last cup from the glass carafe into her mug, and then went about making a second pot. *Throw away the filter and the used beans, but* not *the basket. New filter, more ground beans, rinse the carafe, pour the water into the machine.* She could do this now.

"Shall we work on your self-defense moves today?"

Could she do that?

"I'm meeting with Lily at the Fortune headquarters later this morning, but I have time to practice your moves."

Her self-defense moves. That was what she needed, right? Self-defense. If she could protect herself from hurt, then maybe she could protect herself from the way Emmett's disinterest was bothering her.

"Okay. Sure. Why not? How about now?"

She met him across the mat with less than half a cup of caffeine in her system. It was enough, though, to get her pulse jumping.

"Are you ready?" he asked.

She glowered at him, annoyed by how attractive she found him and how it bothered her that he wasn't attracted back. "Just try to take me on."

He frowned. "Didn't I tell you not to have that macho attitude? These are last-resort moves, remember? Your first options are to avoid dangerous situations or run like a rabbit."

Too bad. She was feeling pretty macho right now, if macho meant mean. A man should not call a woman his "light," make perfect, heart-stopping love to her, then turn around and treat her like a near-stranger for the next few days. She bent her knees a little, then curled the fingers of both hands in a little "gimme" gesture.

"Just try to take me on," she said again.

Emmett rolled his eyes. "I feel the animosity rolling off of you. What's up?"

"You'll feel more than animosity when you try to take me down," she spit out. "I'm in a mood, Emmett."

She hoped that wasn't a smile she saw twitching at the corners of his mouth. "I can see that. And what kind of mood is it, exactly?"

Hurt. Confused. Disappointed. Frustrated. Okay, really, really frustrated. Because he'd ignited this sexual fuse inside of her and then only given her that one opportunity to explode. And there he stood, as cool as you please, as if he didn't feel that desire still burning between them.

She could go after him for that.

Why didn't he want her anymore? And how could she achieve his same level of detachment?

"My mood is determined," she told him. If he could pretend nothing had ever happened between them, then so could she.

He shrugged. "All right." In a quick movement, he came toward her, grabbing her ponytail and pulling her forward.

She remembered what to do, even with the quick flood of adrenaline. *Don't pull back. Follow the attacker's energy and step in toward him.* She turned her body so that she was in a stable stance over her feet and at the same time slammed her elbow into his ribs.

Emmett grunted, let go.

She sprang back, breathing hard. "How'd I do?"

He was rubbing his side. "Has anyone ever told you you are one bony woman?"

"Whiner. How'd I do?"

"Great," he acknowledged.

"Then do another one. Try to get me again."

He gave her a wary glance. "Have I created a monster?"

You've created something. She made that little "gimme" gesture again. "Come on, Emmett."

He circled the mat and she shifted as he did, keeping her eyes open to what he might be planning. She was feeling pretty proud of herself but wasn't going to get cocky. However, she was going to show him that she could be as tough, as focused as he was. He would never guess that just watching the play of his muscles beneath his clothes could be distracting if she allowed it to be.

He darted forward.

Thinking about his muscles had been her undoing, because he was too quick for her to move out of reach. He slipped his arm around her head, then pulled in and down. The headlock.

She knew what she was supposed to do. The same as with the hair grab—she was not supposed to fight the attacker's movement, but follow it and use his energy to power her own escape. The technique was to go with the motion and as she did, she was to put both of her hands between her own neck and his arm. She was supposed to roll his arm outward while she let the weight of her body slip her head free of his loosening hold.

It was a good theory. She'd practiced it before.

But now she froze within his embrace, the side of her face against the hard wall of his chest. She could hear his heart thudding against her ear. His scent—that soap she'd used and that shampoo she'd sniffed—wrapped around her just as tightly as his arm.

She loved how Emmett smelled.

"Are you all right?" His eased his hold.

"Don't let go!" She grabbed his forearm as she was supposed to. "Give me a minute. I can do this. I can get away from you."

But what if she didn't want to? What if she wanted to stay against him all day, his warmth and strength surrounding her.

Over her head, she heard him draw in ragged breaths. That was weird, because she wasn't fighting him in the least. She was just standing in his embrace. It shouldn't be hard for him to breathe.

"Emmett—"

"Linda—"

They spoke at the same time.

He started again. "Maybe we shouldn't—"

"I can do this." She would. Tightening her hold on his arm, she attempted to push his elbow out. But he didn't budge, and when she strengthened her grasp, he only held her tighter against his thudding heart.

Frustrated, she shoved her shoulder into his chest, a move coming from her mood and not her previous lessons. But somehow it worked, or kind of worked, because when she did it again, he lost his balance. They fell toward the mat; she was still in the circle of his arm.

Thwack. He landed flat on his back. She landed on top of him.

They stared at each other, both of them breathing hard.

"You hurt?" he asked.

"No. You?"

"No."

But neither of them moved. She had no idea why Emmett stayed supine, but she was out-and-out stunned, because her pelvis-to-pelvis sprawl over him made one thing perfectly clear.

He wasn't as immune to her as he was pretending to be.

Chapter 10

Maybe the meeting on the mat would have gone some-where, but Ricky chose that moment to bang on the guest-house door. Emmett put her away from him in a flash, leaving her to wish the boy a good-morning all alone. The ten-year-old was on his way to school, and he'd stopped to say goodbye. He'd been doing that lately, and today he wanted her to sign a permission slip.

"Permission for what?" she said, frowning down at the half sheet of paper.

"We're going to a bookstore at the mall to hear an author talk," Ricky said. "It's probably going to be dumb, but if I don't get the slip signed, I'll have to sit in a third-grade class and do multiplication tables again."

"What's three times five?"

"Fifteen."

"Seven times eight?"

Ricky rolled his eyes. "Fifty-six."

She had only one more question to ask. "Nine times three."

"Twenty-seven." He sent her a quasi-exasperated look. "Satisfied?"

"Yep. The bookstore it is, then."

He hung around a few more minutes after she'd penned her name on the Parent or Guardian line. She offered him a piece of toast, but instead he exchanged the apple in his brown bag lunch for one of the bananas ripening on the counter. He also snitched a couple of cookies, but she pretended not to see it. Maybe it wasn't motherly of her, but an extra Oreo or two wasn't going to send either one of them to jail.

Finally she waved him off for the bus stop. She stood in the doorway of the guest house and watched him stride away with the rollicking, confident gait of a boy who had extra cookies in his pocket and a field trip to look forward to the next day.

"He could have had Nan sign that slip, you know."

Linda turned to face Emmett. She was glad she was still gripping the doorjamb, because the sight of him in a gray suit, white shirt and emerald necktie made her knees go soft. "You think?" Not what *she* was thinking, not when he looked so sophisticated and so male in his businessman attire.

"He's accepting you."

"Uh-huh." Whatever he said. Emmett's face was clean shaven and she could smell the slight limey tang of aftershave. Some brain-injured people found certain senses were heightened after their trauma, and Linda was just realizing that her sensitive nose might be a side effect of hers. It wasn't something to rue, though, not when she found Emmett so delicious to be around.

What if she said that to him? What if she told him, outright, out-front, straightaway? *I love the way you smell.* Her mouth opened, but then she quickly closed it. That was one of the things they'd worked on in rehab. Acting on impulse, saying the first thing that came into one's head, that was something to be careful about. Normal, uninjured people censored themselves. It was part of the social contract, the counselors had taught them, and she was usually pretty good about remembering it. And wasn't it just plain dangerous to reveal so much of yourself? What if she'd misread everything about that morning in her bed the other day and then that proof of his arousal on the mat a little earlier? He *could* have had a banana in his pocket.

The thought made her smile, but it didn't solve her problem. If you were always second-guessing and censoring yourself, how did you ever signal your wants and desires?

"I'm going to be gone a few hours," Emmett said. "Would you like something while I'm out? I could stop by the grocery store or someplace else."

That was how a woman would send out signals to her man. She'd go to the department store or to a specialty shop and buy something really sexy, some little nothing that said everything she couldn't.

Annoyance flashed through Linda. *She* couldn't do that. She couldn't ask Emmett to bring home satin lingerie, size skinny. And she couldn't see herself asking Nan to make a Victoria's Secret run with her, either.

"I need to drive," she blurted out. "I need to get my license so I can have some independence."

He blinked and took a half step back. "I hadn't realized I was crowding you."

No. No, no, no. She rubbed her forehead, trying to

think her way through the misunderstanding. But it was all muddling inside her head. His great scent, her great lingerie plan, the great-and-growing-greater annoyance that she couldn't do anything about either of them.

"You need your pills." He strode to the bathroom and then the kitchen, and was back in a flash with her pain medication and a glass of water.

It only increased her annoyance and sense of frustration. "I don't need a keeper." She didn't want him to see her as an invalid, an obligation. "I need a driving lesson."

"Fine." The brush of his hands was impersonal as he handed over the water and the tablets. "As soon as I get back from the Fortune headquarters."

Jason hunkered down in the rusty Buick, the car parked so he could see the entrance to the high-rise headquarters of Fortune TX, Ltd. The nearby street sign read Kingston Street and the public park at the end of the block was called Kingston Park, both named for the selfish bastard that had shattered Grandpa Farley Jamison's dreams.

Jason had the urge to get out and spit on the signage, but he couldn't attract attention to himself. He didn't want to miss anyone going into the office building, either. He'd been staking out the place for days, not even leaving the car to relieve himself. Every morning he brought along an empty juice bottle to take care of that necessity.

It didn't matter. He'd take his leaks in the gutter if it meant making his brother Emmett pay.

Sliding his hand in his pocket, he felt the warm metal casing of his cell phone. Maybe he should give the stinkin' straight arrow a call. Just a little jolt to let him know that brother Jason was on the job.

But nah. Let the bugger sweat.

Still, even a conversation with someone from the stupid side of his family gene pool sounded entertaining. Waiting was hellishly boring. Being anonymous while waiting was even more hellishly boring.

Jason was accustomed to attention. Like that architect chick he'd met at the coffee place. He'd liked the way she'd looked at him with her big eyes, all impressed by his act as the grieving but game P.I. But she was probably as duplicitous as the rest of her gender. Think of Melissa. Cheating bitch. She'd thought to double-cross him by starting an affair with Ryan. Jason had choked the life out of her before that could happen.

Of course, then that Nosy Parker reporter had seen him and gone squealing to the police. Just another stupid bitch getting in his way.

He shifted in his seat and glared at the unfamiliar young woman coming down the sidewalk toward him. She'd probably try to get in his way if she could, too. Lifting his hand, he pretended to take target practice at her with his thumb and forefinger. She couldn't see him through the tinted windshield, but he imagined her surprise when he pressed the "trigger" of his thumb, anyway. *Pow.*

The next woman who tried to hamper his plans was going to get it. No more Mr. Nice Guy. He'd let those people go—the egg farmer's daughter and the businessman he'd carjacked—but that was Jason's last good deed. He hadn't been appreciated or treated right, so now the gloves were coming off.

Emmett and whoever else Jason didn't like were going to pay.

A car turned into the Fortune TX, Ltd. entrance. He squinted against the glare, making sure he could get a good look of the driver. And bingo! It had taken four days and four plastic bottles of piss, but he'd just found the man he was looking for.

The straight arrow had gone for the target, just as Jason had predicted.

Damn, he was smart. Now he just had to wait.

It took a couple of hours. But Jason didn't let the time get to him. Sure, he felt the ol' adrenaline kicking in, but it only sharpened his focus. When he finally saw Emmett pull out of the Fortune headquarters parking lot, Jason was ready to trail him.

The San Antonio afternoon traffic was his friend. It slowed down his brother's big SUV but gave enough camouflage in which the Buick could hide. "What is that Sting song?" he said aloud, then hummed a few bars. "'I'll Be Watching You.'"

Emmett's vehicle was heading more toward the center of town. Jason shifted in his seat, spine going a little straighter, to catch his brother making a quick maneuver to take advantage of a stale green left-turn arrow.

"Damn it," Jason muttered, as he was forced to make his own speedy maneuver to keep up. The car he cut off honked angrily behind him and he gave the slowpoke the finger. Didn't the world know it should make way for Jason Jamison?

Emmett was driving faster now, and Jason had to put the pedal to the metal. The piece-of-crap Buick didn't like being pushed—hell, it probably wanted to be pushed, but by human hands—and it coughed and wheezed as it lurched down the street. He was forced to back off in case the noise attracted his brother's attention.

The SUV made another turn and Jason followed. They were in a residential area now, not unlike the 'burb he'd lived in with Melissa the slut. The way she'd decorated the place they'd owned there, he should have known she wasn't good enough for him. She'd hired some snooty designer who'd painted every room in a different jarring color—lime green for the kitchen, fuchsia for the master bedroom. No man could get a good night's sleep surrounded by all that pink.

Not to mention all those sick glass sculptures Melissa had dropped wads of cash to buy. Instead of throttling her, he should have knocked her over the head with one of them. Women. What a waste of time they were outside the bedroom.

"Damn!" Jason had to hang a right on two wheels. Preoccupied with thoughts of the bimbo, he'd nearly missed Emmett's next turn. "Focus," he told himself. "Keep your eyes on the prize."

He had to keep farther back now, because there was even less traffic here and the houses were larger—friggin' mansions. What the hell was his little brother doing in this wealthy familydom? Jason peered down a gated drive, then had to jerk his attention back to the road as Emmett made another series of turns. Jason followed, and then…then it was as if Emmett had disappeared.

"Damn it, damn it, damn it!" Jason slowed to a crawl, swiveling his head for a sign of the SUV. Down one of these other driveways? The houses in this area had large detached garages and he could glimpse the roofs of guest cottages behind some of the large main houses.

Approaching an intersection, he looked in all directions. "There!" he crowed to himself. Just down the block was Emmett's SUV, still on the move. Jason turned, speeding so he wouldn't miss his quarry's next turn. But then, out of a hedge-lined driveway, a white Hummer shot into the street, blocking his path.

Jason stood on the brakes. The Buick burned rubber against the blacktop. A woman rolled down her window, an apologetic smile on her face. She gave him a little wave. "Sorry," he saw her mouth.

It didn't ease his fuming temper. Scowling, he steered his car around the hulking gas-guzzler in front of him to see—

No sign of Emmett. None.

His brother had gotten clean away.

The Hummer driver was behind him. He stared at the woman in his rearview mirror. If looks could kill, she'd be dead. Dumb, stupid bitch. She was blonde, like Melissa. God, how he hated blondes.

The next one who got in his way was going to pay for Melissa, and this greedy Hummer driver, and all the others who'd gotten in his way.

Linda's mood hadn't improved much several hours later as Emmett drove her toward the outskirts of town, looking for a deserted area for her to practice behind the wheel. "How was your meeting?" she asked, trying to sound polite.

"Fine."

She didn't ask what it was about, figuring if he wanted her to know, he would share it with her. Which got her remembering that maybe he didn't want to share anything with her. Frustration again. Disappointment. Annoyance.

When he pulled into the empty parking lot of a half-completed industrial park, she could barely bring herself to look at him. "Ready?" he asked.

"Sure." They changed places, and he told her how to adjust the SUV's driver's seat. He was dressed in jeans and a T-shirt again, but his attitude was as businesslike as his business suit had been.

"Start the car," he said.

As much as she wanted this, she was nervous again. She blew out a breath, then rubbed her damp palms along her thighs. The car roared to life when she turned the key.

She jumped. "This is the biggest car I've ever driven," she said. "I feel like I could climb a mountain in this thing instead of tooling it down the street."

"Why don't you start by moving forward. Put it into Drive."

She did, then released the parking brake.

"Give it some gas."

The pedal was sensitive. She thought she was being gentle with it, but the car shot forward as if pulled by stagecoach horses feeling a whip.

Her foot stamped on the brakes. Even in their shoulder harnesses, she and Emmett jerked forward, then slammed back.

"Damn it," he bit out. "Go easy, okay?"

"I was trying to." She thought the vehicle might be a little like its owner. Big, but touchy, touchy, touchy.

"Do it again," Emmett said. "Remember a little gas goes a long way."

"Fine." Linda inhaled a deep breath, then let her foot press down on the pedal again. The car seemed to buck forward, but then it settled into a slow acceleration. She edged cautiously forward.

"Good," Emmett murmured. "Now take it around the perimeter of the lot. There's nothing around here for you to worry about except for that big pole in the middle."

He shouldn't have said that. Whatever that big pole was for—a flag, a sign to be installed later?—it now seemed to have a magnetic attraction. The circles she made grew ever tighter in its direction. Though she tried widening her path again, she always found herself heading closer to that big piece of metal.

Emmett, though silent, was using the brakes on his side of the car—the imaginary ones that she could see causing the muscles in both of his thighs to strain.

"I'm not doing that bad," she said, glancing over at him.

"Look ahead, okay? Not at me."

She rolled her eyes, but kept driving, trying to ignore the tension rolling off him. But then he winced as she avoided that big metal pole another time.

She jammed on the brakes and was satisfied when his head thunked against the headrest. "Look, if you don't want to help me learn to drive, fine. But I can't take your obvious fear that I'm going to smash into the first inanimate object that crosses my path."

"I don't mind helping you drive." He sounded defensive.

"Yeah, sure. You're over there digging a hole into the floorboards on your side of the car."

"So I'm a little tense."

"You're a lot tense!"

He muttered something under his breath.

"Was that 'woman driver' that you just mumbled?" she said, incensed.

"No! It was, 'Woman, you're driving me nuts,'" he corrected. "There's a distinct difference."

"Oh, yeah?" She crossed her arms over her chest.

"Yes, yeah." He mimicked her pose. "Your way, I'm passing judgment on all the females out there behind the wheel. My way—"

"It's just *me* behind the wheel."

"No. It's you." He sighed. "Goddamn it. Fine. It's you behind the wheel, on the mat, in the kitchen, in the bedroom. You make me tense anywhere that you're around me."

She stared at him. "Huh?"

"I want you every damn minute and I'm fighting a losing battle not to do something about that."

Emmett scowled at Linda, who was gazing at him from behind the driver's wheel as if she thought he was nuts. He felt nuts. She *made* him nuts. The vow he'd made to himself during his lunch with Collin the other day, to cool things between them until the Jason problem was finished, had been sensible. Reasonable. Cautious.

But she made him forget all about playing it safe.

"I'm really mad at you," Linda whispered.

"So you've made clear during our little driving lesson."

"Not because of that, but because you've made me wait."

Half-turned, he watched her put the car in Park, turn off the key, set the parking brake. "Made you wait for what?"

She launched herself from her seat into his lap. His spine thunked against the passenger's door. Her arms went around his neck and he heard the distinct click of the lock being set.

"Wait, wait, wait." His hands grasped her waist in preparation for lifting her off him. But he couldn't do it, because her hip was grinding against his too-ready erection and it felt so damn good.

"I'm waiting for nothing," she said. Her hair brushed his cheeks as she lowered her mouth.

The kiss started sweet. He didn't think Linda had it in her to start with anything less than sweetness, so it was up to him to turn up the heat. For the moment he couldn't think of why he shouldn't. He thrust his tongue into her mouth and slid his hands up her rib cage to cup her breasts.

He loved the little sound she made deep in her throat. It burned through his blood, turning him on. His thumbs rubbed against her nipples.

Her fingers slid into the hair at the nape of his neck. They bit as he found the first button of her shirt and slipped it free. "Emmett?"

There was no one around them. Leaving the headquarters of Fortune TX, Ltd. he'd had the prickly sensation of a watcher's eyes. He'd momentarily regretted his decision to lock up his FBI-issued weapons in Ryan's gun cabinet before moving in with Linda—knowing that Ricky would be in and out of the guest house— and he'd been extra careful as he returned to the Armstrongs, first driving through another residential area clear on the other side of town. He was certain he hadn't been followed to the guest house, certain they hadn't been followed to this deserted parking lot, certain that he couldn't wait any longer to have more of Linda.

"Shh, honey, shh. You'll like this, I promise." He spread the sides of her shirt to find the near-transparent bra beneath. It only took a second to unfasten the front clasp and push both straps off her shoulders.

Naked to the waist and riding his lap, Linda stared at him with those wide, blue eyes. He smiled, letting only the tension touch her, as he let his gaze wander from her pretty, pretty face, down the length of her neck to her fluttering pulse.

Her pink nipples were just a hop and skip from there, and he saw them tighten into darker pink buds under the weight of his gaze.

"It's hot," she whispered. "So hot."

"I know." Dusk was settling around them, but with the car off the air-conditioning was off, too. He punched the window controls, letting the passenger's side down, then leaned the other way to unroll the driver's window. A warm cross breeze meandered through the car, fluttering the ends of Linda's blond hair and brushing across her naked skin. Emmett watched goose bumps spring to life across her delicate collarbone. Her nipples went an even darker pink.

"Cooler now, honey?" he asked, his voice rough.

She shook her head, her hair swirling over her shoulders to cover her breasts. "Hotter."

"I'll help." With his fingers, he lifted the ends of her long hair from her areolas and budded nipples. He saw her fighting against the light touch, her body radiating sensual tension. Then he leaned forward and, without touching her anywhere else, he ran his tongue around and around the stiff crest of her left breast.

She whimpered.

He lifted his head and blew a stream of cool air against the wet tip. Her thighs, straddling his, tightened against his outer muscles. Knowing what she needed, he brought his head to the other breast, lapping at the nipple and then blowing more cool air against it.

"Emmett…" Her lashes fluttered against her cheeks.

"I'm here, honey."

"Not here enough." Her voice broke. "I need more."

He smiled to himself. He needed more, too, but this was so good. Waiting had its uses. His thumbs grazed across the damp tips, and her head fell back. She was so damned beautiful.

He kissed her breasts again, then took one into his mouth, rolling his tongue over the nipple as he played the other with his fingers. She rocked against his lap, rubbing his erection at the apex of her thighs. Heat rocketed down his spine, tightened his legs. He grasped her hips.

"We need to get home now," he said, his voice raw. "We need to wait to finish this until we get home."

She was still riding him with those sinuous, needy movements. "I can't wait, Emmett."

"You can." They both could. It was one thing to play with her pretty breasts in the front seat of a car, but hell, they were adults. They had beds, a whole house to have sex in that was just a few minutes away.

"Don't make me wait."

He groaned, then took her hard nipples between his fingers, applying just the gentlest pressure. "Okay, honey. Okay." He couldn't refuse her, a thought that he stashed away in his mind to worry over later. It was the protector in him that had him going against his better judgment, he told himself now. He was doing what he must to take care of her. He'd bring her to climax.

She slid the warm heat between her thighs against his groin. He caught one of her nipples in his mouth and sucked at it, and she whimpered again, the movement of her hips going wilder. That burn burst through his blood again.

He'd never been with a woman who was so open about her responses. Who held nothing back from him.

It was so damn seductive.

She clutched at his T-shirt with her fingers, and then began yanking it up.

"Whoa, whoa, whoa," he said, lifting his head from her breast.

"Take this off," she said.

"I don't need to take that off." He glanced around the empty parking area. No one was in sight, but he was trying to keep control here. Her fingers on his naked skin could ruin that.

"Emmett, please." The husky little plea in her voice was his undoing. Grabbing the hem himself, he yanked the shirt over his head.

With a little sigh, she pressed her naked torso to his.

He groaned. This wasn't good. Her heart was thudding wildly against his bare flesh, and the silky heat of her skin was setting fire to his. His hands settled on her waist to lift her up, to lift her away, but at that same moment she met his mouth with another of her deceptively sweet kisses.

Coupled with the carnal way her body was sliding against his, *sweet* wasn't innocent, white-sugar sweet, but sticky, caramel, can't-get-enough-of-it sweet. He thrust his tongue into her mouth, and as if she thought his taste was candy, too, she sucked on it.

He almost lost it then, right in the tight fit of his jeans.

His control was lost.

He wasn't waiting anymore, either.

She was soft and pliable beneath his hands, lifting

up, shifting here, moving there, so that he could get her bottom half as naked as her top. He unzipped his fly with shaking hands and pulled out his shaft, heavy and hard and more than ready to lose itself in the melting center of her body.

He directed it with one hand and pushed down on her shoulder with the other. Half an inch from paradise, he froze.

"No. Stop."

"No, don't stop." She made to lower herself farther.

He grabbed her upper arm. "Honey, no. No condom."

She stilled. Her eyes popped open. "No condom?"

He nodded his head with a jerky movement.

She was breathing hard. "In rehab, I went on the Pill. They thought it was best in case of…impulsive decisions like…"

He laughed harshly. "Like this? But it's not just pregnancy—"

"I've been tested for every disease known to man."

"Me, too. FBI protocol. I'm clean, but—"

"But what?"

"But I'm still having trouble getting a word in edgewise around you."

Linda sighed. "I'm sorry." She made a little go-ahead gesture.

He forced himself to look into her eyes instead of at her nakedness. "But you shouldn't listen to some man on this, honey. He could be lying to you, not caring whether he hurts you or not."

"Are you lying to me, Emmett? Are you going to hurt me?"

"No."

"Then love me. Oh, Emmett, just love me."

He groaned, then let her body settle over him.

Emmett, just love me. He stashed that away to worry about later, too. Right now, there was just the absolute perfection of her body over his, surrounding his.

He thrust up his hips, needing more of her, needing all of her, and he didn't stop to worry about that, either.

Now wasn't time for control or time to wait. Now was time for Emmett and Linda, naked with each other, naked to each other. He saw the wonder of that in her eyes and in her cry as she climaxed around him.

And he followed.

Chapter 11

"I'm not a teenager," Emmett groaned to Linda, as he parted her thighs to settle between her legs. "Even if I'm acting like one."

She laughed at him, lifting her body to his. It was dawn, and they were in her bed, making love as they'd done each morning—and each night—since that evening in the parking lot. It had been three days and she was wallowing in every glorious moment of togetherness. "I think I've discovered a new talent," she said, closing her eyes as he rubbed his hard chest against her tight nipples. "I think I'm good at sex."

He groaned again. "You're very good at sex, honey."

His mouth started on a decadent path from her mouth, along her neck, and she tilted back her chin to give him access. Could any woman be so happy?

She was wallowing in that, too, rolling herself in

happiness and not letting any thoughts of problems or the future shadow the past sunny days.

"What are you doing?" She lifted up on her elbows as Emmett slid his mouth over one breast and down her midriff. He lapped at her belly button, and she gasped.

"I've gotta taste all your sweetness, honey," he said, his mouth on the move again. "A girl who's good at sex should know that."

But she was no more a girl than he was a teenager, and it was adult pleasure that burst along her skin and then through her bloodstream as his tongue stroked the soft petals of her body. "Emmett—" The wet heat of his mouth tore her protest away. *"Emmett."*

He held her hips while he helped himself to the uncontrollable responses of her body. She put her hands over his, gripping him, holding on tight until she was riding the waves of pleasure. Her knees folded back as he crawled up her sated body. One thrust and she was tingling again, taking him in with a new abandon.

He lasted just long enough to bring her to climax again, then slid to the side of her body and rested his cheek on her breast. As the sun rose higher, he drifted into sleep. "Don't let me stay under too long," he murmured. "Meeting a man at nine."

"Okay," she whispered, stroking his thick dark hair. It had so fascinated her from the first, and now it was hers to touch at will. Ten years "asleep" and she'd woken to this. To Emmett.

She reached for the notebook and pen on her bedside table.

Today is Tuesday.
Emmett Jamison is tender and sexy and has spent another night in my bed.
I've fallen in love with him.

Linda didn't let herself worry about that, though. She just went about the usual morning routine— shower, coffee, a perusal of the newspaper—until Ricky knocked on the door before leaving for school. He didn't bother with the excuse of the permission slip anymore. He still snitched cookies. She still pretended to look the other way.

She had hope.

As usual, she waved him off when it was time for him to leave, standing in the doorway until he was out of sight. She loved the guest house's small porch. It was bounded by a white-painted balustrade and rails. An old weathered carousel horse was installed in one corner. The sunshine felt so good on her face that she stood there a little longer, her eyes closing.

"Good morning!" A stranger's voice.

Her eyes popping open, Linda jerked back. The man's face was unfamiliar, too. He was wearing khakis and a sports shirt. He carried a duffel bag. "I'm looking for Emmett Jamison," he said.

She stepped backward into the house. Her back bumped against Emmett's front. His hand on her shoulder steadied her.

"Nolan Green?"

The stranger nodded. "Photographer, *San Antonio Express-News.*"

Emmett passed Linda to shake his hand. "This is Linda Faraday. Honey, he's going to take a few pictures of me, okay? I didn't get a chance to tell you."

Because they'd been making love and then he'd fallen asleep. She'd woken him on the way to opening the front door for Ricky. "All right."

He chucked her under the chin. "Get me coffee?"

"Sure." She wanted to ask what the photos were

all about, but didn't want to pry. Being in love with Emmett didn't mean that he was in love with her. "Mr. Green, coffee?"

At the shake of his head, she headed back to the kitchen as the photographer began unpacking his cameras from the duffel bag. She could hear the men talking through the open door. Nolan Green wanted to take the shots outside. "Right here on the porch will be great," he said. "The setting will make you appear more accessible."

"Lawyers aren't usually going for the friendly look," Emmett said.

"FBI agents, either," the other man responded. "I've read the article these photos will run with—about you and the foundation you're putting together in Ryan Fortune's name. We have some archived photos of him that we'll be running with the article as well, I'm sure."

"Good. But I want my photo there, too. And my name front and center in the article."

On her way back to the front porch, the coffee in hand, Linda paused at his words. Emmett, looking for publicity? That seemed odd.

Moving again, she made it to the front porch quickly. He took the proffered coffee. "Thank you." Half of it went down in the first swallow. "Now I know I'll live to see another day."

Something about the light words scared her. She swallowed. "You…you talked to Lily about that foundation idea I had?"

An expression she didn't recognize—guilt?—crossed his face. "That day I went to the Fortune headquarters. We talked out the terms, got the ball rolling, even put together a press release. Both Lily and I did an interview with a reporter at the *Express-News* about it."

The photographer was snapping pictures, so Linda moved out of camera range. "You didn't mention it."

His gaze found hers. "I've been thinking of other things when I'm with you."

And making plans that he didn't want her to know about.

It was confirmed when he shot a glance at the reporter. "Make sure she's not in the photos, okay, Nolan?"

Protecting her again.

From what?

"I'm going to be at the press conference you've scheduled, as well," Nolan said. "Noon on Friday?"

"That's right," Emmett said. "We'll be outside the Fortune headquarters. The TV stations should be on hand, too."

"Fortunes are big news in this town." Nolan said, then hesitated. "Our article might include a sidebar on your brother Jason. Is that going to be all right?"

Emmett shot a look at Linda and shrugged. "I can't control the press."

But he wanted to, Linda suddenly realized. That was what this was about, the photos, the timing of the foundation announcement, the press conference on Friday. He wanted to make a big splash in the press, to attract attention.

One person's attention.

Our article might include a sidebar on your brother Jason.

This was about Jason Jamison.

"Isn't your brother in South America or somewhere?" Her voice sounded high and breathless, but she couldn't help it. "He got away with the ransom money, right?"

Emmett shrugged again, not looking at her. "He's somewhere."

Nolan took his camera away from his face. "I heard the FBI thinks he's still around here. Word in the news-room is that he's been making threatening phone calls to you."

Emmett frowned. "Somebody is talking more than they should."

Linda's heart froze. That sounded like it was true. "No, Emmett, no."

He glanced over at her, then glanced away. "Don't worry, Linda. Nothing's going to happen. Not to you, not to Ricky."

Because Emmett Jamison, FBI agent, was still on the job. The interview, the photos weren't about the foundation, they were about his other job, as a federal agent. As the man determined to stop his brother.

The man she'd fallen in love with was setting him-self up as bait.

Linda didn't know what to do. Her brain was mud-dled again and she didn't trust herself to voice her fears and objections to Emmett just yet. Leaving him with the photographer, she wandered toward the main house.

The cook let her into the kitchen and set her up with a comforting cup of tea at the long farmhouse table in the middle of the room. A small TV broadcast one of the network morning programs. She let the newscaster's voice drone over her as she sipped at the tea and tried to get her new bearings.

She was in love with a man who would do anything to capture his brother.

How could she possibly stop him?

A few minutes later, Nancy Armstrong came bustling in the kitchen, and she smiled as she caught sight of Linda. "Good morning! I'm so happy to see you. Why have you happened by on this lovely day?"

Lovely day? Linda glanced outside. She supposed the sun was shining, but it didn't feel very warm and bright inside her soul. Inside, she felt jittery and unbalanced and…afraid. "Emmett was having some photos taken for a newspaper article, so I decided to get out of the way."

Nan poured herself a cup of tea from the waiting pot and pulled out another chair at the table. "Well, good. We don't have enough chance to gab, you know."

"Gab?"

"Girl talk. Fashion analysis. Possibly even celebrity gossip. My bridge club was canceled this week and I'm in desperate need of feminine conversation. With Dean retired and home all day long every day, I spend too much time answering questions like where I keep his socks, the stapler, and have I seen the strawberry jelly. It doesn't matter that they're in the same places they've been for the last forty years. He doesn't look for them himself first. He just asks me where I'm hiding them."

Despite her mood, Linda found herself smiling at that. She knew that Dean Armstrong had been a successful CEO before his retirement. To think that he was stumped by locating his socks! "I don't feel so bad about my own mental lapses now."

Nan took a sip from her tea. "It appears that you're making incredible progress."

"I think I am." She still had her little routines and

her props, but her notebook, which had kept her mind straight for months, was now more of a diary than a necessity. "The headaches are coming less often. I don't need as many naps as I used to. A few more lessons behind the wheel and I think I'll be ready for my driver's test."

"You're forging a relationship with Ricky, too."

"He had me sign his permission slip this week," Linda said. "Emmett thought that was a very good sign."

Nan nodded, smiling. "He's recognizing you as his parent."

Something in the tone of the older woman's voice had Linda setting down her teacup and reaching across the table. "Oh, Nan. I haven't thought hard enough about how all this has been for you. You and Dean were his parents for all these years. And now—"

"His *grandparents,*" Nan corrected. "We always made that distinction in our own minds and we tried to in Ricky's, as well."

Linda squeezed the older woman's hand. "You two are the most special people I've ever met. I'll never be able to say how grateful I am to you. To have taken in a stranger's child…"

"Oh, shh." Nan's face was a pleased pink. "The child was no stranger to me the instant I held him in my arms. It's not difficult to love such an innocent little bundle."

"But he wasn't a blood relation." Linda didn't say it aloud, but she still was insecure about the strength of the relationship that *she* could forge with the boy, and she'd given birth to him. It wasn't that she didn't know she should forge it, it wasn't that she would stop trying to forge it, but could an adult and an older child really develop a love for each other?

Could she feel a maternal love for Ricky? Could she be his *mother?*

"Why such a long face?" Nan asked.

"I shouldn't have one," she said. "It's just that sometimes…" How could she express her doubts to the older woman? Maybe she would think Linda didn't deserve Ricky or was trying to pass off the responsibility.

"How are Ricky and Emmett getting along?"

That question had Linda brightening again. She leaned forward in her chair. "Peas in a pod. They like the same kind of pizza, the same kind of pie, the same cartoons. I believe that Ricky is the better speller, but he likes Emmett to help him with his math homework more than me. Apparently my examples can't hold a candle to Emmett's. He creates word problems rife with references to Nintendo games and *Rugrats* episodes that go right over my head."

Nan laughed. "He'll make an excellent father."

Linda fell back against her seat. A father? Emmett a father? Ricky's father? Her husband? Is that where she was hoping her feelings for him were heading? "I've never really thought of him in that way before," she murmured.

Nan raised her eyebrows. "Maybe you should, Linda."

Linda's gaze jumped to the speculative gleam in the older woman's eyes. "I don't— I haven't— We—"

"Don't leave me to start bringing up hemlines, Linda, or, God forbid, make my only interesting conversation today to be about where I have secretly stashed Dean's tackle box."

"Emmett's just helping me out because of his promise to Ryan." That was how it had started, anyway. And she couldn't know if he had any deeper feelings for her than that, despite the fact that they'd been sharing a bed. Despite the fact that he'd soothed her head and opened her heart and reminded her what it felt like to be a woman. To be wanted, desperately.

"I've seen the way he looks at you, Linda. Like you're the sun and he's basking in your light."

Oh, if that were true. But she'd seen it in his face when they made love. He never closed his eyes. He loved to watch her as he touched her, taking in her responses in a way that made her only burn hotter. He'd given her so, so much.

"He's a dark man," she said, half to herself. "He's seen things that have made him retreat to the shadows."

"You're right," Nan answered. "But you can take his hand and pull him out. That's what people do who care about each other. What lovers do. They lift each other up."

Could she really do that for Emmett? Did she have what it took?

Your bravery, your fortitude make me believe in goodness again. That it can win. Emmett had said that to her. And that was what Nan was talking about.

But it was scary to take on the job for a lifetime, wasn't it? As scary as taking on the care of Ricky.

"It's frightening to love someone," she whispered aloud. "What if… What if I mess it up?"

"The bad news is, you're right, it's frightening." Nan's smile was gentle. "The good news is, a woman doesn't have any choice."

Linda frowned. "That's the *good* news?"

"It takes the angst out of the situation, don't you

think? If you are destined to love, you might as well get used to it."

Destined to love? Where did destiny fit into all of this?

Somewhere, she thought. For a woman who had been "woken" by way of a miracle—no one had another explanation—she had to believe in the touch of something larger than herself…didn't she?

A phone rang. "I'll get it," Nan said to the cook, and reached for the wireless phone on the countertop.

So if she was bound to love Emmett, Linda thought, then there was no reason to stew about it. That he was setting some sort of trap for his brother…now *that* she could stew about. And more. She'd talk to him about it. Share her concerns, her fears, maybe even her love.

This evening, in the quiet privacy of the guest house, she'd share her true feelings with him.

"Oh, no!"

The distress in Nan's voice gave Linda a jolt. She jerked her head toward the older woman, trying to read the trouble in the expression on her face.

"Which hospital?" Nan asked, her cheeks pale.

Hospital? The word grabbed Linda's heart and shook it like a dog with a bone.

"Is he conscious?"

He who? Her heart rattled inside her chest again. Ricky? She tried to say his name aloud, but nothing came out of her dry mouth with its thick, heavy tongue. Had something happened to Ricky?

No, no. Paralyzed by something she'd never felt before, she stared at Nan. Is this what motherhood was, then? This dry throat and shuddering heart and sudden outcry from the soul that said, *Please, if something is wrong, take me instead!*

The call ended, and Nan placed the phone back in its cradle. Linda stared at her, desperate to hear the news.

She turned toward Linda. "It's Dean's brother. He's had an accident."

Air whooshed out of Linda's lungs. "Oh. I'm sorry." She put her hand over her calming heart. "What happened?"

"They think he broke his leg and injured his spleen, but they're running some other tests." She hesitated. "His wife wants Dean and me at the hospital."

"Of course," Linda said, already rising from the table. "Can I help you in any way?"

"They live in Utah," Nan explained. "We're going to have to be away from the house for at least a few days."

"Oh, okay."

Nan met Linda's gaze. "Can Ricky stay with you while we're gone?"

"Certainly." It was an automatic response. It was what she had to say, right? But her heart was jumping around again. If Ricky stayed with her in the guest house for a few days, with her and Emmett...

She'd see just how maternal she was.

She'd see how she and Emmett and Ricky could operate as a family.

She wouldn't be alone with Emmett, which would give her time to reconsider telling him how she really felt about his plan to lure his brother...and how she really felt about him.

Funny how she could be so nervous and so relieved all at the same time.

Jason kept going farther afield for his morning cup of coffee. In a small café, he ordered an extra—he'd drink it cold midmorning during his Fortune TX, Ltd.

stakeout—then took them both toward the grouping of tables. All of them were taken, but knowing there might be long hours ahead in the Buick, he opted to share an open space on a ratty loveseat. He had a free hour before he figured he needed to be watching the high-rise headquarters.

The flabby fortysomething man beside him was reading the *San Antonio Express-News*'s local section. Jason sipped at his coffee and glanced over, then coughed as the hot liquid went down wrong.

Emmett's photo was on the front page. And Ryan Fortune's.

The two people he hated most in the world.

He shot a look at the newsstand by the first register, but it was empty of newspapers. The one by the second held only the friggin' *New York Times*. Who cared about the Big Apple when the Big Pain in Jason's Ass was featured front and center on the Texas paper?

Shifting in his seat, he tried to get a look at the text beneath the photo. He could only make out a word here and there—*Lily Fortune, foundation, federal agent.*

Jason was surprised they were talking about Emmett and federal agent in the same article. What kind of federal agent could Emmett be? He had to be crying himself to sleep every night, wondering where his older, smarter, wilier brother had got to. Emmett hadn't been able to find him. Emmett couldn't find his ass with both his hands.

Feeling smug, Jason leaned back against the cushions and sipped at his coffee. Whatever the article said, it wouldn't change a thing. Jason was going to be the one to find Emmett and then…*kaboom.*

Still, his curiosity was piqued. He squinted at the article again, then looked up when the paper rattled.

Over the top, the fat guy holding the thing was staring at Jason.

Not letting a beat go by, Jason smiled, then gestured at the newspaper with his cup. "Sorry, I was intrigued by the front page article. Something about the Fortunes?"

The man folded the paper over to look at the story in question. "Oh, yeah," he said. "Ryan Fortune's widow and some of his relatives are creating a charitable foundation in his name."

"A charitable foundation?" Jason's voice was mild, but inside he felt the rage start simmering again. The Fortunes were planning on handing money out to the sniveling and to the stupid, when the old bastard Kingston hadn't been moved to give so much as a penny to his Grandpa Farley! "Must be nice to have so much extra cash."

Jason's two mil was looking punier and punier. They'd probably give twice that much to a bunch of Girl Scouts or some goddamn endangered eggplant.

"They're good people, all right," Fatty said. "They bought all new band uniforms and instruments for my kid's middle school music program."

See? *See?* The Fortunes were playing the role of Harold Hill for a bunch of loser kids, when they could have funded a political dynasty by backing Farley all those years ago. How much had been stolen from his grandfather! How much had been stolen from Jason himself!

"So who's heading up this foundation?" Jason asked, though he knew the answer already.

The man held up the newspaper to display the front page photo. "Emmett Jamison. Some connection of the Fortunes."

"Ah." Jason nodded, his eyes roaming over the photo. "Does the article say where this Emmett is living?" Not that he'd take Fatty's word for it. He was going to get his own copy and search the article himself.

The other man shrugged. "I didn't see nothin' about it."

Jason stopped himself, just barely, from rolling his eyes. The fathead had "nothin'" for brains, that was obvious.

Fatty was lifting his big butt off the sofa. "You want?" he said, holding out the paper to Jason.

He shrugged. "Sure. Thanks." Then he watched the other man waddle through the café doors before he gave his attention to the article. Despite his obvious dimness, the fat man hadn't been wrong. It was a charitable foundation that Emmett was putting together and there wasn't any mention of his brother's current residence.

Jason stared down at the photo of his younger brother. "Damn it," he muttered under his breath. There wasn't a clue in the photo, either. Emmett stood with one hand on a wooden railing. The only thing even halfway distinctive was—Jason leaned closer—half of an old wooden carousel horse. The way the photo was cropped didn't show anything else.

He tapped his fingers on the page. Maybe P.I. Jason had some investigating to do.

It was a woman manning the classifieds desk at the *San Antonio Express-News*. Jason had gambled on it, and he smiled to himself as he pushed a handful of pink bubblegum cigars into his shirt pocket so that their ends peeked out.

Then he mussed his hair a little, pulled out a shirttail, and finally approached the plain, thirtyish woman across the counter.

"Can I help you?" she asked. There was a stack of forms in front of her, as well as a jar of sharpened pencils.

"I hope so," Jason said. He gave her a wide, yet tired smile. "Congratulate me. I just had a baby last night. Well, not me, of course, but my wonderful wife."

God, he was good. The woman melted, her shoulders going soft. "Oh, how terrific. Congratulations."

His gaze flicked behind her, to the neat desk and its fake wood nameplate with gold-toned letters. "She's perfect. Ten fingers, ten toes, a whole bunch of hair. We named her Katherine."

The counter lady's eyes rounded. "That's my name!"

Jason let his eyes widen as if he couldn't believe what he'd heard. "You're kidding! We're thinking of shortening it to—"

"Katie. That's what I've been called since I came home from the hospital."

"Katie." Jason pretended to try it out. "I like it. Katie." He reached into his pocket for one of the bubblegum cigars. "Here you go. From my Katie to you."

The woman beamed at him. "Thank you. Now, what can I do for you?"

"Have you ever had a baby, Katie?" She wasn't wearing a ring and she was plain enough for him to believe she never would.

"No." She shrugged, going a little pink in the face. "Not yet, anyway."

"Well, I realize now that birthing is a big job—and one that I could never do. You women have all my admiration."

More smiles from plain Kate.

"So I want to give my wife a very special thank-you gift. A special thank-you for my perfect, very special Katie."

The real Katie was lapping this stuff up. "Something you've seen in the classifieds?"

"Oh. The classifieds?" He looked around as if he wasn't aware what department he'd wandered into. Playing the dumbass didn't come natural, but he'd do what he had to. "I didn't realize…"

"Well, maybe I can still help you," the woman offered. "Is it something you saw in one our advertisements?"

"No. In one of the photos accompanying an article." He pulled the folded sheet out of his back pant's pocket and spread it out on the counter. "My wife saw this carousel horse and decided she just has to have one for our Katie. I was hoping you could tell me where this photo was taken so I could talk to whoever owns it. If they don't want to sell theirs, maybe they could tell me where I could purchase one just like it."

The woman squinted at the grainy image of the half horse. "It's kind of hard to see."

"Not to my wife it's not," Jason assured her. "She thinks it's the most perfect thing for our most perfect daughter."

Newspaper Katie bit her lip. "We're not supposed to give out that kind of information. Not that our department would even know the address you're looking for."

"Oh." Jason put a crestfallen expression on his face. "I was *so* looking forward to telling my wife that I had a lead on the gift she wants most of all in the world— after our little girl, of course. Our Katie."

This Katie bit her lip again. "I could call a friend of mine in Editorial," she said, lowering her voice. Her gaze shifted left, right. "You couldn't tell anyone how you found out."

Jason took one of the bubblegum cigars and with it crossed his heart. "Don't worry. I'll make up some story."

Chapter 12

Today is Thursday.
Emmett is in his bed because Ricky is camping out in Emmett's room.
Get up, make breakfast, get Ricky off to school.
Confront Emmett about his plan re: Jason.

Linda knocked lightly on Emmett's door on her hurried path to the kitchen. "Ricky, wake up and get dressed for school. I'll have your breakfast ready in just a few minutes."

There was a mumbled response, and Linda grimaced. He'd stayed up much too late the night before; she could hear it in his grumpy voice. She'd known it then, too, but nervous around Emmett and her awareness of her feelings for him, nervous about her responsibilities as Ricky's full-time mother for the next few days, she'd been hesitant to cause any friction.

Instead of putting her foot down, she'd given in to his pleas. The boy had fallen asleep in a chair and Emmett had carried him to the foam mattress and sleeping bag set up in one corner of his room. Linda had hidden away in her own room at the same time. Her poor night's rest—so different from the previous nights when she'd slumbered in Emmett's arms—had caused her to sleep past her usual wake-up time. They were already running late.

She started the coffee and then retrieved the newspaper that one of the main household staff placed on their small front porch every morning. Hesitating a moment there, Linda put her hand on the weathered carousel horse and took a few calming breaths of the warm morning air. Juice and cereal. A brown bag with a peanut butter and jelly sandwich, banana, some chips, Oreo cookies and a box of juice. She could remember these things.

Ironing! She'd almost forgotten that. She'd promised Ricky she would iron his shirt before school this morning. Anxiety set in as a low-level headache at the base of her skull. She ignored it as she dumped the newspaper on the kitchen table and then tapped on Emmett's door again.

"Ricky? Are you up? I'm going to iron your shirt now." At his next grunt of response, she hurried back to the kitchen and set up the ironing board and plugged in the iron. His shirt was hung over one of the kitchen chairs.

As she waited for the iron to heat up, she poured the OJ and a bowl of cereal and set them on the kitchen table, then quickly made Ricky's lunch. Next, she attacked the shirt. And attacked was the right word. It was so small, with a little collar and a three-inch bumpy button placket at the neckline. The side seams wouldn't lay straight. She struggled on, however, the heat of the iron making her feel flushed and sweaty.

Just as she decided she'd done her best, Ricky walked into the room in his long khaki shorts, socks and sneakers. "Your shirt," she said, holding it up.

He looked at her through his long blond bangs. And scowled. "I hate that shirt. It's dumb."

Linda blinked. "This is the shirt you laid out last night. The one Nan packed for you. It's the shirt you wanted me to iron."

"Well, I hate it. I look dumb in it. Everybody will say I look dumb in it." There was a surly curl to his upper lip.

The headache at the base of her skull started pounding like a tom-tom. "Did you bring a different one? Or you could go up to the house—"

"There's no time! You got me up late." He grabbed the shirt and shoved his head through the neck opening.

By the time he stuck his skinny arms though the holes and jerked down the hem, she was holding out his juice. "Here you go." Maybe the Vitamin C would put him in a better mood.

"I don't drink juice." He kicked out the chair and sat in front of the cereal. "I'll just eat this."

Linda swallowed down the glass of juice herself. Maybe it would put *her* in a better mood. While she knew it was Ricky's tiredness that was talking, it didn't help that she knew she was the one to blame for it. She should have sent him to bed earlier. Would she ever get this mother thing right?

Ricky had only a few minutes to get going in order to meet the bus. He wolfed down his Cheerios, brushed his teeth with such speed that certainly potential cavities had to be snickering with glee, then tried to grab his lunch off the countertop. His swipe sent the bag and its contents tumbling to the floor. The juice box exploded. The sandwich slid out of its plastic bag, landing on the growing puddle of juice, where it gathered up the liquid like a sponge.

She knelt down to tend to the mess. "This will just take a second to clean up. Then I'll make another lunch."

"I don't have time!" Ricky snarled. "Can't you bring it to me later? At school?"

"I don't know. You know I can't drive and I'm not sure if Emmett will be able to—"

"What kind of mom are you?" Ricky's eyes glittered with tears. "You can't get me up on time. You can't make a good breakfast. You can't bring a lunch to school. You know what? As a mom, you…you…you suck!"

Then he ran out of the house, slamming the front door behind him.

Linda stared after him, then stared down at the mess on the floor. *Bam, bam, bam* went the thump in her head.

Bam-bam, bam-bam, bam-bam. It doubled its primitive rhythm. Over its thudding beat, she heard the shower going in the bathroom. So that was where Emmett was. Good. She didn't want another witness to the scene between her and Ricky. She wished to God that she hadn't been there herself.

She wished…she wished…

As a mom, you…you…you suck!

"I wish I wasn't Ricky's mother."

There. She'd said it. Out loud, even. And Linda held her breath, waiting for lightning to strike.

No woman should even think such a thing, should she?

Still waiting for a cataclysm, she cleaned up the mess on the floor, made another lunch for Ricky, then poured a cup of coffee. Not knowing what else to do, she sat down at the kitchen table with it, and by habit, unfolded the newspaper. There was Emmett, front and center, looking less like a foundation director and more like the forbidding federal agent he still was. Then she read the article and figured out why. Emmett wasn't just setting a trap and setting himself up as bait for his brother Jason; he was taunting the other man.

A sidebar about the case against Jason was peppered with quotes from Emmett, all which could be summed up in four simple words—*come and get me.*

Staring at the paper, she didn't hear the footsteps over the tattoo of the drums in her head. When a hand touched her shoulder, she whirled and stood in all one motion, her back slamming against the nearby wall.

Her stomach jittered and her heart pounded along with the ache in her head. The threat from the man confronting her was undeniable. "No," she said. *"No."*

Emmett pushed his hand through his damp hair. "No, what?" he asked Linda. She was hugging herself, and her face was pale. "I'm sorry I startled you."

She shook her head. "No."

"What's the matter, honey?" Emmett stepped toward her, ready to pull her into his arms.

Her head shook again, and she sidled farther away. "Stay away from me."

He frowned. "What's going on? What happened?"

"You happened to me, and I don't like it anymore. I don't want it. I don't want you."

Stunned, he stepped back. "What the hell are you talking about?"

"I want you out of the guest house. Today. Now."

He couldn't believe what he was hearing. This wasn't the woman who had been spending night after night in his arms. The woman who had shone the sun into the corners of the darkness inside of him. "What is it? What's changed everything?"

She gestured at the table and the newspaper spread upon it. "You're going to hurt me."

His gaze flicked to the page she'd been reading, then back to her face. "Linda, honey, you're going to be all right. Jason isn't going to hurt you. He doesn't know about you. He doesn't know where we're living."

"I'm afraid of *you*. It's time for me to think about myself. To protect myself. I've been through one disastrous relationship and lost ten years of my life because I fell for the wrong man. I'm not going to take that chance again."

Emmett tried to clamp down on his own rising temper. "Don't compare me to Cameron Fortune. He was an egotistical opportunist. Hell, I'm not out to take advantage of your innocence and your trust. I think I might lo—"

"Don't say it!" She recoiled. "Don't say that word."

"What has you spooked?" He couldn't figure out what had happened. "We've been so good together. Why is the woman who has been so courageous, day after day after day, backing away from what we could have now?"

"Who is that woman? I know for sure she's not any good at motherhood. I only know for certain who I used to be. A bad secret agent accountant. A lousy judge of men."

"You were a lonely kid who made a mistake!" Emmett would like to yank Cameron Fortune out of his grave and make the man abase himself to this beautiful woman who was still reeling from all the ways he'd hurt her. "But it doesn't have to affect *us*."

"Aren't you listening? How do we know I won't screw this up, too, just as I've screwed up everything else? There won't be any 'us.' How can there be, when I don't even know *me*?"

Oh, God! Oh, God! Emmett froze, his anger dying. That was it, then. That was really it.

An aching sense of loss rushed in to take its place, filling the void that he'd just begun to think might actually hold a heart after all.

He'd worried about this when they'd moved so quickly into each other's arms. He'd worried that what she'd felt for him would turn out not to be real, but a figment of her recovery. But damn, it hurt to be right this time. It hurt so much.

She was truly awake now, though, and she was seeing that the dark and desolate wasteland inside Emmett wasn't a landscape she wanted to live with for the rest of her life.

Who could blame her?

It seemed like a hell of a sentence to him, too.

Linda didn't remember ever having liked housework, but it gave her something to do during the long morning and endless afternoon. Working with a determined frenzy, she cleaned the entire guest house, including the room where Emmett had slept when he wasn't in her bed. His belongings were gone from the closet and the dresser drawers, and she changed the sheets, trying not to think of his hard muscles and tanned skin.

In the bathroom, she was distracted by the forgotten bottle of shampoo he'd left on the high window ledge in the shower. She climbed inside the porcelain tub and wrapped her fingers around it, then uncapped the bottle and brought it to her nose.

Emmett. Oh, Emmett.

Closing her eyes, she breathed in the memories. His kindness in the grocery store that very first day, his patience on the mat in the workout room, the way he laughed with Ricky and rooted on the boy's soccer team. *He'd make an excellent father,* Nan had said. Linda hoped he'd get that chance.

It was hard to let go of her own hopes for him, but she recapped the shampoo and put them away as she put away the bottle beneath the sink. Someday he'd find another woman—a woman who could be a good mother, a woman who was whole, instead of the mess of parts that was Linda. The mess of parts who couldn't risk not loving well enough and then losing her heart when she lost him.

That was all she'd been able to think of when she read the article in the newspaper. Her fear for him had demonstrated just how much she loved him. She'd realized that her love for Emmett was so intense that this half-broken Linda wasn't strong enough to withstand potential heartbreak. He was bound to get tired of her weakness and disability eventually. It was better to break it off clean and quick, or else the pain would only get worse.

Though she didn't know if it could get any worse. She sank onto the living-room couch and buried her face in her hands.

A knock on the door startled her out of her reverie. She jerked her hands away from her face and automatically started for the door. Then her steps slowed. Emmett coming back?

Her hands pulled open the door without her permission. No one was there, until she dropped her gaze. Gleaming blond hair. A streak of dirt across one cheek.

"School's out already?" she asked Ricky.

He brushed past her. "It's after three."

She checked her watch. The day had gone quicker than she'd thought. Sheesh. She couldn't even keep track of the time. "Did you get lunch?" she asked, following him toward the kitchen.

His backpack landed on the middle of the table with a big *thwump.* "Yeah, my teacher said you'd called the office and made sure I could buy lunch even though I didn't have any money with me."

"I'll send the cash with you tomorrow." She reached for the brown bag still sitting on the countertop and held it up. "Do you want to eat any of this now?"

He frowned. "What's that?"

"The lunch I made after you ran out of the house."

"Oh." His hand swiped it from hers. "Thanks. But why didn't you bring it to school?"

A real mother would do that, she finished for him. "You know I can't drive. Not yet."

He fished out the cookies, naturally. Linda bit her bottom lip. The school lunch had likely been less than nutritious. And there was the childhood-obesity epidemic. She'd heard about that on TV just the other day. It seemed that during the ten years she had been out to lunch, so had everyone else. Fat-and-sugar-laden foods and supersize portions had helped Americans become overweight.

But Ricky was rail thin. He spent so much time with the soccer ball that she didn't think a calorie had time to settle on his growing little-boy body.

And, after all, she sucked at being a mother.

She let him eat the cookies.

"Where's Emmett?" Ricky asked around a mouthful of Oreo. "I have math homework."

"He's not here. I can help you, though."

Ricky shook his head. "I'll wait until he's back."

It didn't sting that her son didn't want her help. "He's…he's not coming back."

The hand holding the cookie stilled on its way back to his mouth. "What do you mean, he isn't coming back?"

She shrugged. "He's going to be, uh, living somewhere else from now on."

"Living where?"

Linda shrugged again. "I'm not sure."

Ricky dropped the rest of the cookie onto the table and turned his back on her. His shoulders hunched as he shoved his hands into his front pockets. "I was going to invite him to something."

"Oh. Well." She swallowed. "Maybe when Nan and Dean get back in a few days we can find out—"

"It's tomorrow night!"

"What's tomorrow night?"

"It's the father/son school barbecue, okay?"

"Oh, well, I'm sure you don't have to take a father—"

"Of course you do!" Ricky shot her an angry look over his shoulder. "And I was going to invite Emmett last night, but then I—"

Lost his nerve, Linda silently finished for him. Maybe that explained why he'd begged to stay up last night and then why he was in such a terrible mood this morning. He'd wanted to bring Emmett to school with him as his—oh, God—father, but then he'd lost his courage.

"What about Dean?"

"He won't be back in time." Ricky spun around to glare at her. "And I'm not going to bring you."

"Of course not." That didn't sting, either.

"So why did he leave?"

"Well, I…" How much should she tell him? "It was always just a favor to me, to Ryan, really. And sometimes grown-ups—"

"You messed that up, too, didn't you? That's it, isn't it?" There was more hurt than heat in his eyes. "You're always ruining things for me."

Linda closed her eyes. "I don't mean to. Ricky, none of this was my choice. I never wanted—"

"What? You never wanted me?"

The words slid into her heart, cold and deadly. She gasped. No, no. It was bad enough when she thought them, but to hear her son say them out loud…. "That's not true."

It wasn't true. It wasn't, really, that she hadn't wanted him. The truth was, she hadn't wanted to fail him.

Just as she was doing. Her brain fumbled for the right words.

"Well, I never wanted you, either," Ricky declared, swiping his bangs out of his eyes with a hand. "I wish you'd never woken up."

These words didn't hurt as much as the others. *You never wanted me.* But her hand flew up to her heart anyway, just as Ricky, once more, flew out of the kitchen and then out the front door.

Bracing herself against the counter, Linda closed

her eyes. She was a failure. A complete, utter failure. *How do I make this right? How do I fix all the things I've broken today?*

She heard the front door open again. She was afraid to let herself hope it was Ricky coming back. *I don't know what to say to make this right. I don't know what to do.*

"Mom?" a thin, young voice said.

Her eyes popped open. Ricky *was* back, his arm held in the grip of a stranger.

"Who are you?" she said to the man. "What are you doing with my son?"

He answered by holding up the gun in his other hand and training it at Ricky's temple. "I'm here to see a man about a horse."

"What?"

"Sorry." The stranger smiled. "Private joke."

"What is it you want?" she demanded.

"A yacht, a house on the beach in Tahiti, satellite TV and radio. But I'm willing to wait for those." He winked at her. "Right now, I want Emmett."

Oh, God. "He's not here."

"No duh, sweetheart. I noticed his car isn't on the premises." The man kicked out a chair and shoved Ricky into it. "He'll be back."

Jason. This stranger was Jason Jamison. It had to be. Linda swallowed hard. "He won't be back. He left for good this morning. I don't know where he went."

Jason frowned. "Don't give me that. I don't like liars, especially when they come in the blonde bimbo variety." He gestured with the hand not holding the gun; it was still trained on Ricky's head. "You sit down, too, sweetheart. We'll all be here together when Emmett gets back."

* * *

Emmett considered heading for the nearest Texas border, crossing it and never going back. He'd had his taste of the sunshine, and it was all he was going to get. Ever. So he might as well find the deepest, darkest hole he could find and bury himself there.

The cabin in the Sandia Mountains. That would work. It was the place he'd taken himself to after Christopher's death and after the Jessica Chandler case had gone all to hell. He hadn't found sunshine or solace there, but his stash of tequila bottles was bound to be still waiting. Drunk hadn't been such a bad way to spend the days. And nights.

He remembered promising his father that he wouldn't go back there again, but that was before he'd lost Linda. Before the light had left his life. All bets were off now. It was a whole different ball game.

It wasn't any kind of game at all.

Noting the gas gauge on his car, Emmett pulled into the next gas station he came across. And then he noted where he was. Red Rock. For some reason, he'd driven on autopilot to Ryan Fortune's beloved Red Rock, Texas.

A blond-haired teenager ambled out of the small office. "Can I help you, sir?" The kid's flop of hair reminded Emmett of Ricky. Pain pierced him, right where he hoped he didn't have a heart. Not only had he lost the woman, he'd also lost the super speller, soccer phenom who was her son.

"Go ahead and fill it up, please," Emmett told the kid. He got out of the car to stretch his legs as the young man put the nozzle in the tank and went about washing the windows.

"You from around here?" the attendant asked.

"Not really. I found this place through Ryan Fortune." Another pain.

"Mr. Fortune!" The kid smiled. "I knew him. He filled up here, every one of his trucks and the luxury cars, too. When he found out I was good at math but thinking about quitting high school, he talked me out of it."

"He was like that."

"He was more than just talk, though," the kid continued, leaning across the hood to squeegee the other side of the windshield. "My dad had taken off and my mom had lost her job at the county library due to budget cuts. That's why I was going to quit school, so I could work at the station full-time and help out with the bills. But Mr. Fortune found my mom a job in the office at the organic egg farm down the road."

"So you stayed in school after all."

"Yep. Graduating next week. I've been accepted at the state college for the fall, and Mr. Fortune is still helping me out. He put four years' worth of tuition in an account with my name on it."

That was Ryan. And that was the kind of work the foundation Emmett had discussed with Lily could continue. He hoped it wouldn't die without him to oversee things. That shouldn't be lost, too.

"Do you know what he made me promise in return?" the kid asked.

"Nothing?"

"No, he wanted a promise, all right."

Of course Ryan would have asked for a promise, because Ryan was big on promises. *Look after Linda for me, Emmett. Do whatever you can for her and her son.* There was pressure behind Emmett's eyes, and he squeezed the bridge of his nose to force it away.

"He asked me to pass it on. Whatever I could do, whenever I could do it. He asked that I would help other people when I could, for the rest of my life."

"That sounds like Ryan."

The kid had his hip against the front bumper and he was looking off into the distance. "I don't know what I'm going to do, not yet. But I'll be thinking of him all of my life. And the day I do my first good deed, I think he'll know it."

That pressure was building behind Emmett's eyes again and he heard Lily's voice in his head. *I want you—Ryan and I both want you—to be happy. To reach out to life, really live the moment, instead of wallowing in all the ugliness.*

That was what he was thinking of doing, wasn't he? Heading for the Sandias where he could wallow in ugliness and unhappiness for the rest of his life.

Leaving Linda and Ricky untended, the exact opposite of what Ryan had asked Emmett to do. That was wrong. He had to fulfill his promise, didn't he? If she didn't want anything else from him, he could at least give her his protection, from whatever distance she required.

"That'll be forty dollars and seventy-one cents, sir."

Opening his eyes, Emmett dug in his pocket for his wallet. "So your mom's doing okay now?"

He nodded. "Yes, thank you, she is. With my dad gone and her job lost, I think she felt overwhelmed. She used to say she thought she was a failure as a mother and as a woman. Not that my sisters and I believed that, but it's how she felt. She was scared, I guess."

Emmett thumbed through his cash and pulled out three twenties as the boy's words echoed in his head.

She felt overwhelmed.... She thought she was a failure as a mother and as a woman.... She was scared.

Was that what happened to Linda today? Did she get scared?

"But the new job helped your mom with all that, is that right?" Emmett asked, handing over the money.

The boy shrugged. "I think it was Mr. Fortune more than anything. He gave her hope. What he did showed that he had faith in her." He ducked his head as if embarrassed. "At least that's what she tells me."

Was that how Emmett had failed Linda? When she needed reassurance, had he run instead of staying to support her?

Had he run because it was easier than believing he could change, that he really had a heart after all? She'd given him so much hope, from that very first moment he'd seen her, and yet he'd not stuck around to give her any back. Damn it.

When she'd doubted herself as a woman and a mother, *he* had neglected to show his faith in her.

"Your change, sir."

Emmett turned toward the kid, returning from the register in the office. The sun was now just low enough in the sky to dazzle Emmett's eyes. It backlit the attendant, making him just a dark shape. A dark shape that looked eerily like Ryan.

"Don't worry," Emmett murmured. "I've figured it out now. I'm going back to her."

"Excuse me, sir?" The attendant shifted and he was once again the rangy blond-haired Ricky look-alike.

Emmett shook his head, then paused. "You know that promise you made to Mr. Fortune?"

"Yeah?" The teen drew out the word, as if regretting telling this man that was now wearing a goofy half smile anything about his life.

"You've just done your first good deed. And I'm certain that Ryan knows all about it."

The kid was staring after Emmett as he drove away. Emmett waved his hand out the car window, then flipped on the radio. Oh, yeah. He *was* doing the right thing.

He hummed along to "Feelin' Groovy."

Chapter 13

Emotions flooded Linda—fear, anxiety, more fear. They slowed her thinking and hampered her instincts. She could only stare at the dark-haired, almost pretty man who held a gun to Ricky's head as she slowly took a seat at the kitchen table.

"It's all right, Ricky," she said, though her tongue felt thick and the words traveled slowly through the molasses-thick air in the room.

The boy's eyes were wide and trained on her face, as if she were the only thing he wanted to see. "Emmett will be here soon," he muttered.

Jason Jamison smiled. "There, I knew it. Your mom's a lousy liar, kid. I knew Emmett wouldn't get away from me this time. I always win."

Linda couldn't think clearly enough to lie. "I was telling the truth. Emmett left for good this morning.

You can go in his room and check. None of his things are here any longer."

He shook his head. "Not buying it, blondie. Once I found out this address, I used the cross-reference phone book at the library. Had to wait until after ten for it to open, but it was worth it. I called the phone number listed for the address and I'm guessing it's someone at the main house who confirmed Emmett was shacked up with you back here."

"No one would tell—"

"Oh, don't blame Hazel the housekeeper or whoever it was. I said I was little brother's boss at the FBI and that I needed to verify the address so I could overnight him some important evidence." He smiled again. "Good ol' Hazel tripped all over herself to tell me he was staying in the guest house but she'd personally ensure anything that came for Emmett would get to him."

And what had come for Emmett was his brother Jason.

Think, Linda, think. Emmett had spent all that time with her going over self-defense, but now his teaching refused to coalesce in her muzzy brain. Wouldn't you know. She was going to fail at this, too.

"Emmett will make you pay." Ricky shot a glare at their captor.

Jason's eyes were as cold as a snake's. "You've got that all wrong, young man. The one who's going to pay is Emmett."

"What's he ever done to you?" Ricky asked, ignoring the urgent message Linda was trying to telegraph with her eyes.

Don't bait him! Sit quietly and let me think of a way out for us.

Of course, the truth was she couldn't think much at

all. Her only plan was the hope that Jason would grow tired of waiting for the no-show Emmett and go away.

"Both my brothers were thorns in my side my whole life. The biggest mistake I ever made was not doing something about them sooner. Listen to me, kid, you gotta take what you want from life and shoot the people who get in your way."

Ricky's eyes rounded. "You're going to shoot him?"

Linda's heart clenched as she watched the truth dawn on the boy's face. This wasn't a TV show or a Nintendo game, Ricky was realizing now. This was deadly serious. The gun was real, Jason's intent was real, danger was real.

Jason glanced at Linda, then back at Ricky. "Who are you two, anyway? Why's my brother hanging out back here with a woman and her kid?"

Ricky crossed his arms over his narrow chest. "He's been making sure we stay away from other people and that other people stay away from us. We have a deadly disease. You get within…within ten feet and we infect you."

Jason hooted. "So now I've got your disease? That's good, kid."

"If you leave now, right now, maybe you won't catch it."

"Nice try." Jason shifted his gaze from Ricky to Linda. "This kid's got a quick mind, I'll give him that. So you tell me why Emmett's been holed up here."

Was there some story that would give them a better chance? What could she possibly say that would elicit Jason's sympathy or send him on his way? Her stupid head could only fuss with the questions and couldn't come up with any answers. The weight of failure settled more heavily on her chest.

"I have a head injury," she said, because the truth was the only thing she thought she could make ring true. "He's helping me get settled."

Jason's eyebrows rose. "Yeah? That sounds like something my sanctimonious straight arrow of a brother would do. But you don't look like a retard."

"My mom's not a retard!" Ricky jumped up from his seat, and so did Linda from hers.

She reached across the table and grabbed the boy's arm. "It's okay, Ricky."

"It's not okay." He threw the man a dirty look over his shoulder.

Jason had backed off a few paces and was looking at them with amusement. "Don't try to suffocate his spunk, blondie. That's what a kid needs to get ahead. Some fire."

"Is that what you have?" Linda asked. "Fire?" With her eyes, she silently urged Ricky back into his seat and breathed a little sigh of relief as he sat back down. She stayed on her feet.

"Yeah, I have fire. The only one in my generation who it was passed down to. It comes straight from my Grandpa Farley, who had political ambitions, political *talent* that would have taken him to the governor's mansion in Austin and then beyond, if that greedy old miser Kingston Fortune hadn't been so preoccupied with keeping all his money to himself."

Linda leaned against the wall behind her and flicked her gaze to the kitchen countertops. Was there something she could use as a weapon lurking somewhere? She wouldn't have time to go for a drawer and then rummage through it for a knife. But what else might there be?

The pad and pen would be fine for a shopping list,

but wouldn't stop an assailant. The lightweight napkin holder wouldn't do much good, either, nor the wad of napkins it held. What she needed was an old-fashioned cast-iron frying pan.

Something Emmett once said coalesced in her mind. *If someone gets into your house, know that any weapons in your home might be used against you.*

Her shoulders slumped. Even if she'd left out a pot or a pan or two, she would have had to proceed with caution. Jason was bigger than she was, and presumably his reactions quicker than hers, thanks to her head injury.

Jason droned on about his grandfather and his own thwarted ambitions as defeat and an acute sense of vulnerability washed over her. Someone else was going to have to get them out of this.

But there wasn't anyone else. There wasn't.

"Emmett's not coming back," she said loudly, interrupting Jason's monologue. She was sick of her weakness, and sick of believing she might come up with some way to get them out of this. It wasn't going to happen. She couldn't protect Ricky or herself.

She wasn't a whole enough woman.

Jason was staring at her. "I don't know why you keep insisting on that."

"Because it's true," she replied, her voice stony. "But I'll stay with you here as long as you like, waiting. Just let Ricky go. You don't need him."

Ricky jerked straight in his chair. "I—"

"Shh!" She made a slashing gesture in his direction with her arm. "Be quiet!"

"Oooh." Jason grinned. "Feisty mama."

She ignored the taunt. "Please," she said. "Let him go and the two of us will wait for Emmett."

Jason still appeared amused. "Blondie, blondie, blondie. Get your story straight. Emmett's either coming, or he isn't."

Linda rubbed her forehead, frustrated and near despair. "Fine. He's coming. But you won't need Ricky."

"Hmm." Jason drummed his free fingers against his thigh. "You mentioned something earlier about checking Emmett's room for his things. Maybe I should do that. In any case, I think it's smart to take a look around, get a lay of the land."

The muzzle of the gun wiggled as he gestured toward Ricky with it. "Get up, kid. We have a reconnaissance mission ahead." His head turned toward Linda. "All three of us, blondie. Get out from behind that table."

At least they were moving, Linda thought as she obeyed. In the kitchen, she'd felt trapped. Maybe somewhere else in the house her head would clear and she could think her way out of this.

Jason waited in the center of the kitchen until she stood beside Ricky. "You two lead the way to the bedrooms."

At the first step, they heard it. Tires on the drive leading to the guest house. All three of them froze.

"Ah, good," Jason said, his voice filled with authentic pleasure. "I'm betting that's my boy Emmett."

Linda thought it was, too. It sounded like his SUV, but she didn't know whether to feel exhilarated or more terrified. Another dose of anxiety muddled her head. "Let Ricky go," she pleaded to Jason. It was the only clear thought she had. "Let Ricky go."

"I don't think I can." Jason gave her another of his sick smiles. "Because your son will make the perfect human shield."

What? The air was thick again, her feet like lead. She shook her head. "No. Please, no."

Jason ignored her. He made a little "gimme" gesture in Ricky's direction. "Come here, kid."

Ricky hesitated. Frowning, Jason leaned forward to grab him.

Time slowed to syrup. Linda stared at the man's hand, at the black hairs on the back of it, at the groping fingers reaching for her child.

Her child.

Her baby.

Her boy.

I'd like to see you, I'd like to see everyone, take a rigorous self-defense course that stresses awareness first, running like hell second and any kind of combat as a last resort.

Emmett had said that.

It was too late for the self-defense course. And running like hell wasn't an option at the moment, either.

Combat was the only option left, and it seemed possible, doable, goddamn preferred, before she let this conscienceless monster touch her son again.

Linda let out a scream of rage. Fueled by a maternal instinct that was ages old and as strong as all the ages of mothers who had come before her, she rocketed forward. Jason, stunned by her screech or by her sudden movement or both, reared back. She darted between him and her son, shoving the boy farther away with one arm. Her other hand in a fist, she slammed it against Jason's wrist. The gun skittered away.

"Run!" she yelled to Ricky, still moving toward Jason. "Run!"

And then, just as all women who had come before her had discovered, male strength could overcome a woman's strength, even a mother's strength. He slung an arm around her neck, choking her in the very type of headlock Emmett had shown her on the mat.

Jason slammed her up against his body and his arm was tight, becoming tighter. *In a real situation, you'll likely be facing someone larger than yourself and certainly more aggressive,* Emmett had said.

She remembered it as she tried to get her fingers around the flexing muscles of Jason's forearm. *Larger than me,* she conceded, even as stars sparkled on the edges of her vision.

But not more aggressive, she decided. Not more aggressive. *Not when my baby's life is at stake.*

With the darkness of unconsciousness closing in on her, she lifted one hand, fumbled to find Jason's unprotected armpit.

Between her forefinger and the first knuckle of her thumb, she pinched with all her fading strength and maternal will.

As he pulled up and parked outside the guest house, Ricky came tearing out the front door.

He stopped short when he saw Emmett, then pointed in the direction of the house. "Stop him!" he screamed. "Stop him, stop him, stop him!"

Adrenaline poured into Emmett's bloodstream. "What? Who?" He leapt out of the car and grabbed hold of the boy's shoulders. "What's going on?"

"Inside." Ricky's face was pale and his arm gestures wild. "Inside. Your brother…my mother."

Oh, God. Emmett sprinted for the open door, then paused. *Think, Jamison, think.*

He looked back at Ricky. If he rushed in, he could make things worse. "Does he—?"

The kid could read minds. "She kicked his gun away, but he has her around the neck."

Emmett's own throat closed. "Go to the main house and call the police," he ordered, his voice harsh. Then, again wishing like hell he hadn't left his own guns locked up in the cabinet at the Fortune ranch, Emmett rushed down the hall, quietly.

He heard his brother before he saw him. "You're all alike, aren't you, blondie? All you stupid, cheating bimbos who don't know your place, who don't know that it's the way *I* want it and no other."

Emmett reached the kitchen. He could smell that sulfur scent of Jason's evil in the air. His brother's back was to him, and he was screaming at Linda, who was sitting on the floor, propped up by the wall beside the refrigerator. There were red marks on her neck and a glazed look in her eyes.

Okay, okay. She was alive. Thank God. Alive.

"I'm winning this time, you get it?" Jason's voice was almost hysterical. "I take care of Emmett, then I won't have to stay in any more cheap motels and drive any more rusty cars."

His pulse pounding, Emmett pressed as flat as he could against the wall and glanced around the kitchen floor. Where was the gun?

"You're never going to get Emmett." Linda's voice was raspy. "Good is what will win, not you."

There was the gun, on the floor by the dishwasher, tucked in the overhang of the lower cabinets. Between Emmett and the weapon was his brother Jason.

All right, Jamison, breathe, he told himself. With Jason still talking, the best strategy was to wait for the police before making another move.

"What did you say?" Jason bit out.

"I *said* you won't get Emmett."

Why the hell was she baiting him? Emmett thought. But it was such a simple answer. To give Ricky time to get away.

"I *meant* that you're just like your Grandpa Farley, as you said. You're just like him because you're both losers. Pathetic losers."

Oh, God, Linda. No. Emmett tensed, ready for anything.

Jason froze. Then he started screeching again. "Shut up, blondie. Shut up."

He jumped toward Linda, then fisted his hands in her shirt and pulled her up. "And don't try pinching me again, you dumb bitch." His hand drew back as if to slap her.

Emmett erupted from his place in the hall and grabbed Jason's free arm. He spun the other man around, taking in the wild eyes and the spittle at the corner of his brother's mouth. He slammed his fist into Jason's jaw.

A blow like that should have felled an angry rhino, but his brother was madder than that…or just plain mad. He went berserk, his body writhing until he'd broken free of Emmett's grasp. But instead of going after Emmett, he was evil enough to turn toward Linda again.

Wasn't gonna happen, Emmett thought, leaping toward his brother once more. He got both hands on his shoulders and pulled him back. Emmett stumbled, his shoulders slamming into the refrigerator as Jason spun and punched his joined fists into Emmett's solar plexus.

Emmett's air coughed out, but still he managed to grab Jason around the throat. The two of them spun, as

Jason got his own hands around Emmett's neck. Now Jason's back was against the refrigerator. It was mano a mano now, each of them trying to choke the life out of the other.

Emmett didn't feel the fingers digging into his neck. He didn't feel anything but an implacable determination. *I have to stop him.* A memory popped into his mind. Three boys in flannel pajamas and robes, running down the stairs to see what Santa had left beneath the Christmas tree. His mental video camera zoomed in on the faces—Christopher's filled with eagerness, Jason's with avarice, Emmett's own betraying a wariness he'd already felt at five years old.

For good reason.

The bat St. Nick had left for him had already been broken in two.

The set of baseball cards left for his big brother Christopher had been torn to shreds.

Only Jason's mitt lay beneath the tree, untouched.

Emmett remembered the hurt and bewilderment on his big brother's face. His fingers tightened.

I'm stopping him for you, Christopher.

And I'm stopping him for you, Lily, and Linda, and Ricky. For you, Ryan, and for all the others whom his evil has harmed.

I'm stopping evil for you, Jessica Chandler.

The sound of sobbing pierced his thoughts. Something was tugging at his elbow.

He turned his head. Linda.

"Don't kill him." She was crying, tears streaming down his face. "He's unconscious, Emmett. You don't need to kill him."

Emmett blinked, looked back at his brother. His eyes

were closed. His hands had fallen to his sides and were as limp as the rest of his body.

"You'll never forgive yourself if you kill him," Linda said.

He looked back at her tear-streaked face. He took in the marks on the silky skin of her beautiful neck and the tangle of her summer hair. Jason had damaged Emmett's own personal sunshine.

"You'll never forgive yourself if you kill him," she repeated. "Please, don't do this. *Please.*"

Emmett released the hold he had on his brother's neck. His gaze dispassionate, he watched the killer that was Jason Jamison slide to a heap on the floor.

You'll never forgive yourself if you kill him.

Linda's words echoed in Emmett's mind. Funny. Because he wondered if he'd ever forgive himself for *not* killing Jason.

A few hours later, Emmett dialed the familiar number. He didn't know whom he hoped would answer the phone. When he heard his father's voice on the other end of the line, he still didn't know. Would this information be any easier to tell his mother?

"It's good news," he said, trying to assure his father. "We've got Jason back behind bars."

The long silence told Emmett that Blake Jamison didn't know how to consider the information, either. "He's alive?" he finally choked out.

"Yeah, Dad. He's alive." No thanks to Emmett. Guilt spread another layer of blackness over his grim mood. "He's in the custody of the San Antonio P.D. Word is he's singing loud and clear about all his crimes, hoping for a plea bargain."

"What kind of plea bargain?"

Emmett hesitated. "The best he can hope for is that they take the death penalty off the table, Dad. I'm sorry."

"I'm sorry, too." Blake's voice sounded tired and near a hundred years old. "Oh, God. How is it that I can I be sorry and be relieved and be sick about this all at the same time?"

"I don't know, Dad." Emmett didn't know anything more than he had the day his father had found him at the shack in the Sandia Mountains. His soul felt as if it had been sucked back to that place, even though the shell of him was walking and talking here in San Antonio.

"Was…anyone else hurt before he was back in custody?"

Linda. Ricky. *Me.* "No one died. But he scared the hell out of a ten-year-old little boy, and they took his mother to the hospital." He hesitated, then decided that making it pretty wasn't going to help his parents. "Jason was coming after me and he attacked the woman I was staying with, Linda. He choked her and slammed her head against the wall before she was able to break away from him." The pinch, he thought dully. He'd overheard her telling the cops that she'd given Jason the pinch he'd shown her. At least he'd done something for her, besides bringing his maniac brother down upon her. Besides making her serve as witness to the ugliness that was inside of him.

"They took her to the hospital to check out her injuries."

His father made a noise that sounded like a swallowed sob. "It never ends," he whispered.

"No, Dad," Emmett said gently. "It *has* ended now. It has really, truly ended this time."

"I'll tell your mother that," Blake said. There was a long pause. "This woman, this is the Linda whose son your mother has been perfecting her pie recipes for?"

"Yeah." Even the thought of that couldn't make Emmett smile. He supposed he wouldn't ever smile again. "Linda is the mother of Ricky."

"Well, you tell her…you tell her for us that we're sorry, all right? You tell her we are praying for her complete recovery."

"Okay, Dad." Emmett grimaced. "I'll do that." It was a lie. He wouldn't be seeing or talking to Linda again. His relationship with her had ended, too. Really, truly ended.

Chapter 14

Emmett found, however, that he couldn't leave well enough alone. Though he promised himself he wouldn't see Linda face-to-face, he had to go to the hospital himself to make certain she was going to be okay. He made a call to his cousin Collin to meet him there.

His cousin's face was the first he saw as the glass hospital doors automatically opened for him. Collin, who was purported to so closely resemble him, didn't look the least bit bleak and somber—just how Emmett felt.

Though his cousin didn't smile, Collin's handshake was congratulatory. "It's good. It's good to get Jason back where he belongs."

"Yeah," Emmett said. "Good." Whatever the hell that meant.

"I called ahead to Lucy," Collin went on. "Your Linda is on the third floor."

"She's not my Linda."

Collin shot him a look. "Whatever."

"Did Lucy say how she is? If I just knew the prognosis, I wouldn't have to go up there."

Collin was already striding for the elevator. "Lucy didn't tell me that. She said third floor, and that's where we're going, buddy."

Shoving his hands into his pockets, Emmett followed. Coming to the hospital had been unnecessary, he knew that. But his feet wouldn't turn around and head back out to his car.

The elevator ride was brief, the walk to the third floor lounge even briefer. As he stepped inside the pale yellow room, a voice yelled out his name.

"Emmett!" A body hurtled toward him and leapt up.

He had just enough time to catch a little boy in his arms. Ricky's own arms closed around Emmett's shoulders as if they'd never let go. "I knew you'd come," he said. "I knew you'd come."

Over the boy's blond hair, Emmett met the gaze of a female police officer. "He's been checked out," she said to his inquiring gaze. "He's fine. We're still waiting to hear on his mother."

"She'll be fine, too," he found himself murmuring against the boy's soft hair. "Your mom's going to be just fine, I promise."

The boy buried his head against Emmett's neck. "That's what Nan and Dean said, too."

He glanced around. "Are they here?" The older couple would be the natural ones to provide the reassurance the little boy seemed to need right now.

Ricky shook his head. "They're trying to get on a plane. They said they'll be back tomorrow morning."

Emmett cast a glance out the window. Night had just

fallen. "Let's sit down, ace." Without letting go of the boy, he found a seat and settled Ricky on his lap. "Have I introduced you to my cousin Collin? He's CIA."

That got the boy to loosen his hold on Emmett a little. He glanced up at the other man. "No kidding?" He seemed to remember his manners and held out his hand. "Nice to meet you, sir."

Collin shook it, then sat down on the adjacent chair. "I heard some of what you went through today, Ricky. When you grow up, we could use a good man like you. We always need people who can face scary things and keep a level head."

"Yeah?" Ricky looked from Collin to Emmett. "What do you think?"

Emmett thought he had never known the bittersweetness of a child looking at him with such hero worship in his eyes. Sweet, because it promised there might be love, too. Bitter, because he didn't deserve an ounce of it. "I think you'll make a fine decision for yourself when the time comes, Ricky."

"Are you hungry, Ricky?" Collin asked. "My fiancée works here and she's told me what's deadly and what's delicious in the downstairs cafeteria. I could take you there and get you the good stuff."

Ricky shook his head. "Thanks, but no. I need to wait right here with Emmett. The doctors are going to come and tell us how my mom is doing."

Collin gave a little smile. "Yeah, I see that the two of you have to wait right here. Together."

Emmett shot his cousin a look. "Maybe you could go track down Lucy and see if you can goose any more information loose, Collin. I'd like to…to get out of here as soon as possible."

"You're not leaving?" Ricky's arms tightened on

Emmett. "We can't go anywhere until we see my mom and know how she's doing."

Emmett didn't know what the hell to say to that. "I'm here right now, ace." He patted the little boy's shoulder. "Right now, I'm right here."

Ricky settled against his shoulder. "Yeah."

Collin stood and shook his head a little as he stared down at Emmett and the child who was snuggled up against him. "Your mom would get a kick out of a photo of this, cuz. *I'm* getting a kick out of it."

Ricky's chin dug into Emmett's chest as he tucked himself closer. "She's making me a pie," he said, his voice drowsy. "Me 'n Emmett like the same kind of pie."

"'Me 'n Emmett,'" Collin repeated.

The Emmett half of "me 'n Emmett" scowled. "Don't go there." Untangling himself from the kid was imperative, that was certain. "Instead, go find Dr. Lucy, okay?"

With a two-fingered salute, Collin went on his way. Emmett watched after him, noting the other man's long, jaunty stride. He'd always had the long stride, but no one could ever have used the word *jaunty* to describe hard-ass Collin Jamison. But he was jaunty now, his whole being cheerful.

God, how had his hard-edged military man of a cousin become *cheerful?*

But the answer was obvious. He loved, and he was loved in return.

Earlier today—was it just today that he'd been at the gas station in Red Rock?—he'd been determined to get that same sort of cheer for himself. He'd been deter-mined to go back to the guest house and show Linda that he had faith in her, in what they could be together.

He'd been prepared to wait as long as it took for her to believe him. He would have waited forever.

But he no longer believed he deserved her.

Winter was back, inside him and about him.

He was in love with Linda—that hadn't changed, would never change. But now she'd seen the ugliness that was Jason, the ugliness that was inside Emmett himself. *You'll never forgive yourself if you kill your brother.* He knew she would want to keep her distance from him.

That was okay, he understood it. He wanted to keep his distance, too. From everyone.

He shifted the boy on his lap. The regular breaths that were exhaling against his neck told him that Ricky had fallen asleep. Exhaustion was a common aftereffect of an adrenaline rush. Emmett rested his chin on top of the child's head and let his own eyes drift close. He'd just take a brief nap....

Emmett's vision was terrible. He couldn't understand it. He'd never worn glasses in his life, but he could use a pair now. The dim light didn't help and he used his hands to feel his way through the maze of corridors. His heart was pounding and his mouth was dry.

He was so damn afraid.

Not for himself, but for someone else. He tightened his grip on his gun, but then felt only flesh. Astonished, he looked down. Where was his gun? Why didn't he have his gun?

His anxiety redoubled. His breaths sounded loud and ragged in the oppressive dark.

For some reason, he broke into a run, bouncing against the walls that he couldn't see. There were usually sick, noxious smells here, he remembered. Smells of terror and blood and death. But this time he smelled fresh air. Yes. That was what he was running toward. A way out of this living grave.

Around another corner, and he was in that empty room. A figure stepped out of the shadows. Emmett jerked his gun toward it—but he didn't have a gun. He didn't need a gun.

It was Christopher. It was always his big brother Christopher, but this time he brought with him more scents of fresh, clean air. A light opened up behind him.

Christopher held out both his hands to Emmett.

What was in them? The tape? It was always the tape. Emmett tried stumbling back, but that light was growing behind his brother, and its warmth attracted him like a magnet. "Christopher, what's going on?"

Christopher didn't speak, he only smiled. It was a wide smile, a happy smile. Jaunty. Cheerful. Good.

His brother held out his hands closer to Emmett. And when he looked down at what was in them, he had to blink to make sure he wasn't dreaming. But of course he was dreaming. Of course he was.

One of his brother's hands gripped a little boy's unbroken bat.

The other held a fan of unblemished baseball cards.

Emmett looked back to his brother's face. Still smiling, Christopher nodded once, then turned to go. Toward the light.

"Christopher!"

His brother kept on going.

"Christopher!"

His brother didn't stop.

"I miss you, Christopher. I…I love you."

His brother was nearly swallowed by that bright light. But now he turned, waved once and then returned to his original path. Deeper into the light.

Emmett could have sworn there was a young woman walking beside him now. Emmett could have sworn it was Jessica Chandler.

"Emmett." A hand jostled his shoulder. He was having another dream, he thought, trying to rouse himself. Linda was having to wake him again. He would tell her it wasn't another nightmare, though. He would tell her he was in love with her.

"Emmett."

"Linda?" he murmured, opening his eyes.

It was Collin. They were in the hospital waiting room. One of Emmett's legs had fallen asleep thanks to Ricky's slumbering weight.

Collin hunkered down to meet his gaze. "Linda's ready to see you and Ricky."

The door of the private hospital room opened and a blond boy and a dark man stood in the doorway, hand in hand.

Maybe not hand in hand, Linda thought. It was more Ricky clutching Emmett's long fingers, and Emmett not having the heart to break the grip.

It was clear from the expression on his face that he didn't want to be here.

Anxiety flooded through her, trying to seize control of her brain, but she held on to her thoughts in a grip as ruthless as Ricky's on Emmett's hand.

Like her son, she wasn't letting go of him.

Her gaze dropped to her little boy's face, and she smiled. "Can a mom get a hug from the best kid in the world?"

He made a running leap from the doorway to the bed. "Thank goodness the rails are down," she said, laughing as she felt him close his arms around her.

The hug was brief, but heart-wrenchingly sincere. She blinked away the tears in her eyes as he pulled back to look into her face.

His eyes rounded as he took in the marks on her neck. "Wow, Mom. Wicked bruises."

Mom. Thank you, God, she was this little boy's mom. "Yes, well, I'm going to have to do some serious scarf shopping."

Ricky lifted a hand toward her face, then stopped. "I just washed them," he said. "They're clean."

"I don't care if you're clean. I just care that you're here, with me."

He touched the scrape on her cheekbone with a gentle finger. "They said you have a goose egg on the back of your head." A shadow darkened his eyes. "You…you won't go to sleep on me again, will you?"

She caught his hand and held it, hard. "They already gave me something to make me drowsy, but it's not going to be like before. I promise." When her son didn't look convinced, she glanced up at Emmett. "Can we arrange a meeting with the doctor, do you think? I have the impression my boy needs to hear the diagnosis for himself."

"Sure," he said, already turning. "I'll—"

"I didn't mean right now," she amended hastily. She was afraid to let him get too far away from her. There was already a distant look in his eye.

Emmett leaned his shoulder against the doorjamb. Halfway between coming and going, she thought with a sigh.

"They got him in jail already, Mom," Ricky said, even as he found the TV controls that were attached to a nearby cord. "He's never going to hurt you again."

She watched his head bend over the remote. It looked

beyond complicated to her, but Ricky probably thought it nothing more than another version of Game Boy. "He's never going to be able to hurt you again, either, Ricky."

He shot her a quick glance. "He didn't hurt me."

"Maybe not physically, but being scared is a kind of hurt. Isn't it, Emmett?"

He started. She'd been aware of him staring at her and Ricky as if they were candy in a locked shop. It gave her hope. She had to have hope.

"I… What did you say?"

"I was telling Ricky that being scared is a kind of hurt, as real as a scrape or a bruise or a goose egg on the back of the head."

Emmett looked uncomfortable. "Sure."

Ricky frowned. "Emmett wasn't afraid. He ran right into the house when I told him about Jason. He didn't have a gun or nothing. Emmett's never afraid."

Linda raised her eyebrow at the man still standing in the doorway. He looked grim and forbidding, and not a little bit scary himself, but she had to remember that he'd come back to her. She had to remember that look in his eyes when he'd peeled his brother off her. She'd recognized it. It was the determination of someone who wasn't going to lose the one he loved.

She was sure that same look had been in her eyes when she saw Jason reaching for Ricky.

She touched her little boy now, because she could. "Tell me, Emmett, is that right? Are you never afraid? Were you never afraid today?"

"Not for myself." He looked surprised that he'd said the words. His gaze jumped off her face and switched toward the window and the darkness outside. "Though I've been afraid on other assignments, Ricky, that something would happen to me. That I would be hurt, or worse. So I understand that. A courageous person is courageous because he *is* aware of the dangers around him."

Oh, he would make a terrific father, Linda thought. Strong and honest.

"But today you weren't afraid for yourself," Ricky pointed out. "You just said."

Emmett's gaze brushed over Linda's face, then went back to the window. "Today, I was terrified that something would happen to your mother. Pretty much how I guess she felt when she went after Jason in the kitchen. She wasn't worrying about herself then. She did that because she loves you."

Linda's heart tripped. And then tripped again as Ricky turned his head to look at her.

She cleared her throat. "How'd you know about that, Emmett?"

"I told him," Ricky said. "I told him everything that happened while they took Jason away and before the ambulance came for you." He took a breath. "That's why you did it, huh, Mom? You went warrior lady on Jason because you were trying to protect me."

"Yes." And that fierce strength that she'd found inside herself had let her know that forever, for all time, she was Ricky's mother. Really and truly, to the core of her heart, Ricky's mother.

"You…you love me?"

"Oh, *yes*." She gathered her boy close, holding him against her heart. "I love you now. I'll love you always." Tears came to her eyes as she realized she'd never said the words to him. She'd never *felt* the words until today. But that was okay. Because the love she had for Ricky wasn't any the weaker for it.

"I love you, too, Mom."

It was the first time he'd said those words to her, too, and she let herself sob at the joy of it. Finally, she lifted her head to stare into Ricky eyes. Her family. He was her family. She smiled.

"You look funny when you cry," he said.

She laughed. "I suppose I do. Sorry."

Ricky grimaced. "It's not a bad funny. I kind of like it."

"Good save," came the dry comment from the door. Another man was standing there, beside Emmett, a man who looked remarkably like him. "He's got way more innate charm than you do, cuz," this man said, nudging Emmett with his elbow.

Emmett's grim expression didn't change. "Linda Faraday, meet my obnoxious cousin, Collin Jamison."

He smiled at her. "Glad to see you're feeling okay. Your son here didn't want to leave the waiting room until he saw you for himself, but I thought he might be interested in a cheeseburger, fries and a shake about now. I'm almost hitched to a med student on the staff here, and she assures me that they're the best on the cafeteria menu."

Linda raised her brow at Ricky. "What do you think?"

He hesitated. "I'm hungry, but—"

"My Lucy has made arrangements for you to stay in your mom's room tonight, Ricky. So you can get a quick bite and then get back up here and settle in. Your mom's going to need someone who knows how to work that TV remote control."

"Okay, then," Ricky said. He grinned as he bounced off the bed and headed toward Collin Jamison.

Linda smiled to herself. Another man who was going to make a darn good dad someday.

Her son and the other man exited the hospital room, leaving her facing Emmett. "Would you mind closing the door?" she asked.

"All right." He placed his fingers on the handle. "I'll say goodbye, then."

"No!" She cleared her throat as the anxiety collected inside her once more. "I mean, um, no, I have something to say to you. Ask you. Discuss with you."

Oh, God, she was doing that nervous babbling thing.

Emmett narrowed his eyes, but shut the door and then drew closer to her bed. "What is it?"

What was it? What could she possibly say to mend the rift between them? "I want to apologize for yelling at you this morning. For, uh, basically ordering you out of the house."

He shrugged. "That seems like a million years ago."

"Still, I apologize, all right?"

"Okay."

Oh, great. There was nothing between them at the moment, no spark, no current of awareness, nothing but a huge pit of awkward silence. But she had to soldier on. "Why, um, were you coming back to the guest house this afternoon?"

He blinked. "What?"

"Why were you coming back? Did you have something to say to me, or…?" She stared at him, willing him to take the opening she'd given. The whole time the doctors were examining her, she'd gone over this in her head. Why had Emmett come back to the house?

From that look in his eye when he went after Jason, she had been hoping she knew.

He just stared at her.

Linda closed her eyes. Squeezed them tight. What now?

"Honey? Sweetheart?" The mattress depressed as Emmett sank onto it. "Are you having another headache? Shall I call the doctor?"

She opened her eyes, taking in the concern on his face. Ten years hadn't made her any smarter at this man-woman thing, but it should have taught her not to waste time waiting to get smart.

She swallowed. "I don't think the doctor can cure the problem I'm having, Emmett. I don't think I want him to, anyway. I love you, Emmett Jamison. I'm in love with you."

He froze. "You—" He shook his head, as if trying to dislodge a strange thought. "You couldn't. You don't."

"I can. I do."

"No." There was a frown between his dark eyebrows. "You've seen the ugliness, the evil that is my brother. You don't want that to touch you."

"He won't touch me. Jason's not a threat to me anymore."

"But you saw what *I'm* capable of. The darkness that lives inside of me, as well."

She shook her head. "Emmett, there's sadness inside of you because of what you've seen and experienced. I can help with that. Ricky can help with that. Our love, our family that we make together can help with that. But there's no darkness inside of you."

"You don't know…if I love you back." He looked away.

"But I do. I saw it on your face when you were trying to protect me from Jason. You were fierce because you love, Emmett, not because you're bad."

He muttered something.

"Don't try to deny it. You said it yourself. You told Ricky you ran into the kitchen terrified for me. That you thought it was the same way I felt when I was protecting him…because I loved him."

Emmett muttered again. "Me and my big mouth."

"Why won't you give me that love?"

He looked at her now. "Because I don't want to be the shadow on your sunlight."

Oh, God. "I need your love, Emmett. I thought I didn't deserve it, either. I thought I wasn't whole enough for you, strong enough, but I was wrong. And you're wrong, too. Love can never be a shadow."

She put her hand on his arm. "You said you'd be my first daylight man. And I insist you be my last."

He broke then, taking her in his arms. "Linda, Linda." His mouth found hers, and the kiss was wet with both their tears. He lifted his head. "When I moved in with you, I thought you needed me. But the truth is I need you."

Smiling, she cupped his face in her hands.

"We'll shine on each other," Emmett said fiercely. "For the rest of our lives, we'll shine on each other."

Today is Sunday, the Fortune family reunion.
Get up, shower, put on the pretty new sundress.
Get Ricky and Emmett into their party wear.
Remember to thank God for love and family and
the fact that you woke up and found them both.

Ricky glanced at his mom's open notebook. He hadn't meant to read it, but she'd asked him to retrieve her watch from her bedside table and his gaze had caught on his own name.

He didn't think she'd mind. She loved him and told

him so something like a billion times a day. In the middle of doing something else she'd look up and ask, "You know what, Ricky?"

And though he would know exactly what she was about to say, he let her say it anyway.

"I love you, baby."

She was going to have to cut out that baby stuff, but he'd decided to be generous and not mention it until his eleventh birthday. Emmett had explained it to him. Mom had missed out on all those *I love yous* and *babies* and needed to work in ten years' worth of them ASAP.

As long as she didn't do it in front of his friends, he could handle it. He doubted, though, if she could keep them to herself during the Fortune family reunion. Ricky sighed. *What're you gonna do?*

When they made it to the Fortune ranch—which looked pretty even to him, with its wads of pink and purple flowers and white party tents set up all over the place—he found out that *I love yous* were being tossed around like rice at a wedding ceremony he'd seen on TV. There'd been a lot of weddings among the Fortunes in the past few months. It could kinda make a guy sick, except his mom and Emmett and he were going to have their own wedding coming up. He'd told them, no penguin suit! But his mom had sniffled and he'd found himself caving.

Emmett didn't like the idea of a penguin suit, either, but they both liked the idea of pleasing his mom.

"Ricky, please come over here. There's some people I'd like you to meet." That was Lily, who wore a big smile and these long beaded earrings that caught the sunlight.

He walked over to her, but Emmett and his mom came along, too. Ricky knew what this was about.

They'd prepared him, but still it felt like the first day of school and the moment before the shot at the doctor's office put together.

His throat felt sticky as Lily introduced him to her son, Cole, and to Holden and Logan Fortune. All three were Ricky's half brothers. He had a half sister, too, Eden, and she looked friendly and normal enough for someone who was married to a real, live sheikh. They all smiled, actually, and said they were glad to meet him and hoped to get to know their little brother better and he said he would like that.

The surprise was, he meant it.

It was weird, finally knowing all about his past. His biological father—that's what his mom said they should think of him as—was Cameron Fortune, who also was the dad of Cole, Holden, Logan and Eden. His mom said she thought she'd loved him, but it was all hazy for her since it was pre–brain injury. So they'd decided to focus on the present and the future, with the exception of letting him know that he was a real Fortune. Lily said she hoped it would make him feel more… He thought the word she'd used was *secure.* He'd even gone to visit another sort-of relative, Susan Fortune, who helped kids with weird stuff going on in their lives.

She used to live in California, but now she'd moved to Texas and was running her hotline thing for kids from here, because she'd gotten married to Ethan and he lived on a nearby ranch. Between Ricky and Susan, they'd figured stuff out. Basically, he had a lot of people who loved him and wanted to be in his life. Nan and Dean, Lily, the Fortune half brothers and sister. His mom, of course. Emmett's parents, who were here today, too, along with a pie Mrs. Jamison said was just for him. And he had Emmett.

After his mom, it was Emmett who made him feel okay about things. He'd told Ricky he didn't have to feel fine about everything all at once. "You ever feel weird, you come talk to me and we'll work it out together."

Ricky could talk to his mom, too, of course, but it was cool to have a father-type around. Emmett had told him he could call him whatever he wanted, and Ricky had a plan about that. Once the three of them said "I do," then he was going to start calling Emmett "Dad." Guys in penguin suits had to stick together.

"Ricky!" It was his mom this time. "Come meet someone else."

It was a little kid, a girl, with black hair and these huge brown eyes. She was younger than Ricky, by three or four years, and he could tell by the way she was sitting so still in a chair that she wasn't your everyday, wiggly first- or second-grader. Ricky knew plenty about them, because he always had to make sure they didn't go tearing across the street when he was on traffic patrol duty.

"This is Celeste," his mom said. "She's Dr. Violet and Dr. Peter's little girl."

Something about that "little girl" made the teeny kid smile. "Hi," she said.

Ricky nodded. "Hello." His mom was signaling something to him with her eyes, and he thought he knew what she wanted. Emmett was looking at him, too, and Ricky gave a little nod. Emmett called himself a protector, and it seemed he thought Ricky was one, too. It made him feel pretty good.

He sat down next to the little girl. "How's it goin'?"

"Good," the little girl said, peeking at him from beneath these thick dark eyelashes. "I'm learning how to walk again. I'm okay at it, but not ready for the Olympic track team." Her big eyes looked up at her dad, Dr. Peter. "My daddy says I will be able to run someday. Now I swim. Do you swim?"

"Yeah. I do."

They didn't have much more to say to each other, but Ricky continued to sit beside Celeste. The sun made him feel a little lazy. There were other kids around, yelling and laughing while playing hide-and-seek. Maybe he'd go do something with them later. Right now, it was pretty good next to this quiet little girl. Before his mom woke up, when she was asleep in the nursing home, he used to sit quietly with her sometimes, too.

His mom was full of life now, though. She was talking to Celeste's mom, Violet. Dr. Violet wanted to go back to work part-time. His mom was going to be doing that, at the Fortune Foundation that Emmett was setting up. Another couple came up to join them and they started talking about work, too. The grown-ups thought it was way-out funny that this Kyra lady was her husband's boss now.

He shared a speaking glance with Celeste and shrugged. Guess you had to be there.

There was another round of hugging and kissing when more people joined the group that included his mom and Emmett. Ricky had given up trying to figure out how they were related to him. The latest couple was Vincent and Natalie. Everybody screeched when Natalie said she'd finally been given a promotion at the newspaper where she worked. No more fluff pieces, she said, whatever those were.

There was more screeching, when Natalie told everyone she was pregnant. The loudest screech came from Amy Fortune, who said she was having a baby, too, in September. Natalie's husband, Vincent, said he was giving her the first of the five hundred babies he'd promised her. At that, Ricky shot an aghast look at Emmett. "Five hundred?" he mouthed.

Emmett shook his head and leaned down. "An exaggeration," he murmured, his hand on Ricky's shoulder. Ricky liked the feel of that hand. Emmett's other hand was on the back of Ricky's mom's neck, under the hair he was always saying was "pure sunshine."

Ricky had to admit it was pretty. And it made him feel good to know that Emmett thought so, too. Sometimes Emmett got a sad look on his face and Ricky figured he was thinking about his brother, that mean, sick guy Jason. Then his mom would shoot Ricky a glance and the two of them would go to work on Emmett. His mom would go for kisses, and Ricky would go for a football tackle. In no time, Emmett would be smiling. They both knew how to make him happy.

Later on at the party, Ricky stuffed himself with food. Barbecue, corn, a mound of coleslaw. He thought he was the only kid in the world who liked the stuff, but that was what made him special, right? His soccer coach told the team they should eat as many vegetables as they could.

Plus, it meant he could have double desserts. He took his second piece of cake, walked away from the crowd and climbed onto a nearby fence rail to eat it. He'd plowed through about half when he noticed this old guy sitting beside him. He looked kinda like Ryan Fortune—well, he really looked *a lot* like Ryan Fortune, but that didn't mean much since so many people at the reunion were part of the Fortune family. Probably some cousin twice replaced. Or was it removed?

Ricky looked over at him. The guy was smiling, so Ricky smiled back. "Hello."

The old guy's smile got bigger. He had kind of a glow about him that could have been creepy, but wasn't. "Hello, Ricky. Having a good time?"

"Sure."

The man nodded. "I'm glad. It's a good-time kind of day."

Ricky looked out over the crowd of people. He'd seen some tears a time or two, when Ryan's name had been brought up and how he was missing from the party, but Lily had insisted on smiles and good memories, not sad ones.

"It's a strong family, Ricky," the man went on. "A family that comes together when they need each other. That's something to appreciate."

Ricky forked up another piece of his cake. "Yes, sir."

"And it's important to appreciate them. To appreciate the love they have for each other, that they have for you. It's important to enjoy every second of your life. You'll remember that, right?"

"Sure." Ricky's gaze roamed the crowd again and he found his mom's bright hair, and then Emmett beside her, looking dark and strong and sure. They turned their heads toward Ricky and waved. He waved back with his fork.

Then he saw Lily standing nearby, looking at him, a sad smile on her face. Or maybe she was looking at the old guy. Ricky turned his head to check—and saw that the man was gone.

Hmm. Frowning, he looked around, trying to see

where the man had disappeared to. He was nowhere in sight.

But Ricky's mom and his almost-dad were waving to him again. Their arm movements said they wanted him close.

Ricky slid off the rail. That sounded just right to him.

* * * * *

FAMOUS FAMILIES

YES! Please send me the *Famous Families* collection featuring the Fortunes, the Bravos, the McCabes and the Cavanaughs. This collection will begin with 3 FREE BOOKS and 2 FREE GIFTS in my very first shipment—and more valuable free gifts will follow! My books will arrive in 8 monthly shipments until I have the entire 51-book *Famous Families* collection. I will receive 2-3 free books in each shipment and I will pay just $4.49 U.S./$5.39 CDN for each of the other 4 books in each shipment, plus $2.99 for shipping and handling.* If I decide to keep the entire collection, I'll only have paid for 32 books because 19 books are free. I understand that accepting the 3 free books and gifts places me under no obligation to buy anything. I can always return a shipment and cancel at any time. My free books and gifts are mine to keep no matter what I decide.

268 HCN 9971   468 HCN 9971

Name _____ (PLEASE PRINT)

Address _____ Apt. # _____

City _____ State/Prov. _____ Zip/Postal Code _____

Signature (if under 18, a parent or guardian must sign)

Mail to the **Reader Service**:
IN U.S.A.: P.O. Box 1867, Buffalo, NY 14240-1867
IN CANADA: P.O. Box 609, Fort Erie, Ontario L2A 5X3

* Terms and prices subject to change without notice. Prices do not include applicable taxes. Sales tax applicable in N.Y. Canadian residents will be charged applicable taxes. This offer is limited to one order per household. All orders subject to approval. Credit or debit balances in a customer's account(s) may be offset by any other outstanding balance owed by or to the customer. Please allow 4 to 6 weeks for delivery. Offer available while quantities last. Offer not available to Quebec residents.

Your Privacy- The Reader Service is committed to protecting your privacy. Our Privacy Policy is available online at www.ReaderService.com or upon request from the Reader Service.

We make a portion of our mailing list available to reputable third parties that offer products we believe may interest you. If you prefer that we not exchange your name with third parties, or if you wish to clarify or modify your communication preferences, please visit us at www.ReaderService.com/consumerchoice or write to us at Reader Service Preference Service, P.O. Box 9062, Buffalo, NY 14269. Include your complete name and address.

FFBPA11